THE MYSTERY OF THE HELLENISTIC HOARD

THE THREE INVESTIGATORS

IN

THE MYSTERY OF THE HELLENISTIC HOARD

BY

ELIZABETH ARTHUR
& STEVEN BAUER

BASED ON CHARACTERS
CREATED BY ROBERT ARTHUR

Hollow Tree Press 2025

CONTENTS

1

An Unexpected Meeting

Pete Crenshaw hunched forward on his bike, pedaling hard. It was a beautiful June morning in southern California. The sky was a deep cloudless blue that lightened at the horizon, and Pete was in a particularly good mood as he headed for the Rocky Beach Animal Rescue Center for a few hours of volunteer work. After that, he'd be off to a meeting with Bob Andrews, Jupiter Jones, and Mallory MacLeod at Three Investigators Headquarters.

The four of them had just gotten back from a case in the Napa Valley that had involved a search for a hidden treasure – Pete's favorite kind of case! – and Pete couldn't imagine there would be another like it any time soon. But Bob had gotten a number of e-mail inquiries, one of which might possibly be The Three Investigators' next case, and they were going to discuss them later today.

Pete was in a good mood because he'd spent the morning with his father, who was back in town for a few days. Martín Crenshaw was a set construction supervisor, currently working on a film about the U.S. Army Signal Corps during World War II. This morning, Pete's father had told him that the Corps had been responsible for communications among the various U.S. and Allied fighting forces on land, on the sea, and in the air.

"Imagine how important that was," his father had said.

"How did they do it?" Pete had asked.

"They used radio signals mostly," his father said. "Like the walkie-talkies you and your friends use, but a lot more sophisticated. They had to keep inventing new ways to get messages through, to keep ahead of the Germans."

"So I bet they didn't use signal flags," Pete said, grinning. The previous summer, he and Bob had been held captive on a boat in the course of a case, and Bob had jerry-rigged a distress signal using flags hung out of a window.

Martín Crenshaw laughed. "No," he said. "They had to use secret signals. So no Morse code either."

"Wow!" Pete said. "I haven't thought about that in a while." Morse code was a pretty neat way of communicating, he thought. In the code, every letter in the alphabet was converted to a series of dots and dashes, and they could come at you pretty fast.

All Pete had ever learned in Morse code was SOS – three dots followed by three dashes followed by three dots – *dit dit dit, dah dah dah, dit dit dit.* That was the universal signal for trouble or distress and it stood for either Save Our Ship or Save Our Souls, no one seemed quite sure – but originally, when a ship at sea was in trouble, it had sent out an SOS. Now SOS was universally recognized as an urgent request for help.

"I don't know if you knew this," Pete had told his father, "but when Bob and Jupiter and I were kids – before Jupiter even founded The Three Investigators – we used to send SOS signals to one another with our walkie-talkies. Jupiter, of course, became an expert on Morse code. I bet he still remembers all of it."

Mr. Crenshaw had laughed. "I bet he does," he'd said.

As he biked along, Pete was also thinking about an e-mail Bob had recently gotten which *hadn't* been asking The Three Investigators for help. It had been from a boy they'd met a couple of years ago on a case they'd been on in Florida – a boy named Christos Markos, who he and Bob had been trapped with in an underwater cavern, and with whom they'd found a bunch of Spanish doubloons.

They hadn't seen him or talked to him since the case had ended, but Bob told Pete that in his e-mail Chris had said that he and his father had moved back to Greece.

Pete had gotten so lost in his thoughts about his father and Christos Markos that he wasn't paying a lot of attention to what was going on around him, so he was startled when a banged-up pickup truck began to pass him on the left. When he turned to look at it, he was even more startled.

He knew that truck! It had been painted a bright yellow – and not professionally. A plywood cap covered the truck's bed. The front fender sported a large rusted dent, and on the passenger side – now passing Pete – was a long continuous crease as though the truck had driven too close to a metal post.

The truck looked even more scratched and battered than it had the last time Pete had seen it, but the yellow paint and the fact that it had been richly decorated with stylized human figures still made it as cheerful as Pete remembered.

"Rafael!" Pete yelled. He waved madly.

By then, Rafael Solares had recognized him as well, and as Pete applied the brakes on his bike and came to a sudden stop, Rafael pulled over to the side of the road, turned the truck off, and jumped out.

"Pete Crenshaw!" he said. He seemed even taller than Pete remembered – three or four inches over six feet, with broad shoulders and a narrow waist. His hair was still jet-black and pulled back in a ponytail and his bronze skin contrasted with the light fringed buckskin jacket he was wearing.

Rafael was part-Chumash and part-Spanish/Hispanic, and Pete and his friends had met him the summer before when he'd enlisted their help with a case involving animal smuggling. He'd been worried that his son Gabriel might have started running with a bad crowd, but luckily, he hadn't. Gabriel lived with his mother in a town near San Diego, but Rafael lived with his girlfriend up near Santa Barbara and had been part of the case in which Bob had hung the signal flags out of the boat window.

Pete put down his bike and rushed to bump fists with Rafael.

"Wow!" Pete said. "It's great to see you! How's Gabriel?"

"It's great to see you too!" Rafael said. "Gabriel's fine. He's going to be spending six weeks this summer with me and Elena. This *is* a coincidence, running into you like this. Now that school's out for the summer – ”

“Hooray to that!” said Pete. Because Rafael was a special education teacher, he also had the summer off – more or less.

“ – I came down to Rocky Beach for a visit. I'm staying with Wally and Isabella for a few days.”

Rafael had lived in Rocky Beach when he was growing up; in fact, he'd gone to Rocky Beach High, where his English teacher had been Wally Tate.

The Three Investigators had met Wally – who was now in his 90s – through Rafael. They had introduced him to Isabella Chang, a retired history teacher they'd met on their very first case the previous summer. Wally and Isabella had hit it off splendidly, and now they were sharing Isabella's house.

“I was planning, of course, to stop by the Salvage Yard,” Rafael said, “so that I could see you all. How's everybody?”

“Terrific!” Pete said. “At the end of last summer, Jupe made Mallory a Special Consultant, so she works with us on every case now.”

Rafael nodded as though he'd known

that was going to happen. In fact, Pete thought, he *might* have known; he was a pretty intuitive dude.

"Actually," Rafael said, "I wasn't just planning to visit. I wanted to consult with The Three Investigators."

"You mean, on a case again?" Pete said, astounded.

"Yes," Rafael said. "Where were you biking to so furiously?"

"The Animal Rescue Center," Pete told him.

"No more capybaras, I hope," Rafael said, laughing.

"No more capybaras," Pete said.

"Well, let's put your bike in the back of my truck," Rafael said. "I can take you, and on the way I can fill you in on the details."

In no time, Pete's bike was secured, and Pete was in the front seat, next to Rafael. Rafael turned the key in the ignition and the truck's engine coughed several times before finally starting. He put it into gear, and they lurched forward and back onto the road.

Pete started laughing. In spite of the fact that the truck seemed to be held together with duck tape and paperclips, Rafael was as calm and serene as always. He was one of the most positive people Pete had ever met, and one of the least excitable.

"I see you haven't gotten a new truck," he said.

Rafael smiled. "No," he said. "I like this one, for some strange reason." Pete didn't know if Rafael was driving slowly because this was how fast the truck went or if Rafael was taking his time so he could tell Pete what he had to say.

"So what's up?" Pete asked.

"I'm worried about a friend of mine," Rafael said.

"Is he Chumash?" Pete asked.

"No," Rafael said, "he's a Classics professor at UC Santa Barbara. His name is Godwin Cuthbert Stonebridge."

Pete was thunderstruck. "What a name!" he said. "I've never known anyone named Godwin," he said.

"I hadn't either before I met him, but he's British," Rafael said.

"What do you actually call him?" Pete asked.

"Mostly Dr. Stonebridge," Rafael said. "He's quite famous in certain circles. He's very proper – he has one of those upper-class British accents – but he's a really nice guy, very open-

hearted and curious. He wanted to know everything I could tell him about the Chumash.”

Pete thought of William Worthington,
The Three Investigators’ friend whom they'd
met when Jupiter had won the use of a gold-
plated Rolls-Royce. It had come with Worthington, who was the chauffeur. He was the
only Englishman Pete knew.

“Dr. Stonebridge is actually an archaeologist,” Rafael went on. “That's why he was
interested in my stories about the tribe; he's fas-
cinated with the past. But mostly he studies the
ancient Greeks. He spends six months of every
year back in the Mediterranean, on an archaeological dig in Greece.”

Pete had met an archaeologist in an
early case with The Three Investigators, but
since he didn't know what a Classics professor
did, he asked.

“Classics is mostly the study of the ancient Greeks and Romans,” Rafael explained,
spinning his steering wheel a little as he turned
a corner.

“Students study Greek and Latin language and literature as well as the inventions
and ideas of the two civilizations and how they
intertwined. Greek culture was really important
in the history of western civilization − that's

where the concept of democracy started. Greeks were the first to assemble books in one place and to put on plays with seats around a stage. In other words, they invented libraries and theaters."

"Wow!" Pete said. "It's amazing to think they actually *had* to be invented. We studied the Greeks a little in 8th grade, but it was mostly about their buildings."

"Tip of the iceberg," Rafael said "They also had very intriguing thinkers. In fact, one of the first things I ever learned about the Greeks – it might even have been Wally Tate who taught me – was that one of their philosophers theorized that the universe was made up of only four elements – earth, air, fire, and water.

"I really liked the idea – both elegant and very simple. I liked how earth and air, fire and water were opposites. Very metaphoric and dramatic. In fact, it seemed to me like something the Chumash would have come up with," Rafael added.

Pete liked the idea too – and since he and his father had seen a movie called *The Fifth Element* together, his head was instantly filled with images from that film – in which the fifth element was life itself!

"The ancient Greeks were also polytheists. They worshipped a lot of gods, instead of just one. Zeus – called Jupiter by the Romans – was the most famous," Rafael said.

"I knew that!" Pete said. "That Jupiter and Zeus were really the same god – the head god, actually. I mean, how could I forget it with Jupiter being one of my two best friends? He, Bob, and I actually know someone who's living in Greece now! His name is Christos Markos. We met him on a case in Florida a couple of years ago, and he was a really big help. He and his father are deep sea divers, but his father got injured. Anyway, they were running out of money, so they moved back to Greece – to some island in the Mediterranean – a couple of years ago."

"It's really a very small world," Rafael said.

"No, it's not," Pete said. "It's enormous! You still haven't told me why you're worried about your friend. How did you meet him?"

"I met him at a party," Rafael said. "I know a very rich businessman named Dimitri Dimitriou who gives a lot of money to worthy causes. He threw a fund-raising party for Special Ed at his estate on the ocean – not far from Santa Barbara – and I met Dr. Stonebridge at the party. Dimitri is Greek –

originally from an island called Naxos. Dr. Stonebridge started his archeological work on the island, so he's known Dimitri for a very long time. They both have a great interest in Greek culture and Greek antiquities."

Rafael looked at Pete as though he were trying to figure out the best way to tell him what came next, and then he just went ahead.

"I don't usually listen to gossip," he said, "and people will say anything about anyone. But three different people at work have told me that they'd heard rumors about Dr. Stonebridge."

This was what they called hearsay, Pete knew – not first-hand knowledge, but it still could sometimes contain interesting information. In fact, it had been a rumor Pete had heard from a boy named Mikey the summer before that had caused him to go to the exotic bird shop where he had first met Rafael Solares.

"These people heard that Dr. Stonebridge has been helping to smuggle antiquities out of Greece and into the United States," Rafael said.

"You mean like stuff he's found when he was doing his archaeology?" Pete asked.

Rafael nodded his head. "That was the

implication. But although I don't know Dr. Stonebridge all that well, I know him well enough to know that he would never, in a million years, be involved in anything like that."

"I know what you mean about those sorts of rumors," Pete said. "Before we even met Chris Markos, we heard that he was bad – a thief and worse. But we could tell right away that he was a good guy and that the rumors were wrong. We helped set all of them straight and cleared Chris's name. And Sir Iain at the Rocky Beach Summer Theatre – "

Rafael smiled. "I knew I was coming to the right people," he said. "Even before you told me The Three Investigators already have a history of rescuing reputations. I don't think Dr. Stonebridge has heard the rumors, but even if he has, I suspect he's not very concerned about them. Which is a mistake."

"I know," Pete said. "People seem to get a kick these days out of ruining other peoples' lives. It's disgusting."

"Especially when the rumors are absolutely false," Rafael said. "Anyway, I'm afraid that one of these days someone is going to call the Classics Department or the police and tell them what they've heard. If that were to happen, it wouldn't be long before Dr.

Stonebridge's job was in danger. Do you think you guys could help?"

"I don't know," Pete said. "We're between cases at the moment, so I'll totally bring it up. We're having a meeting in a couple of hours about what we should tackle next."

He was quiet for a minute, staring out the window. They were close to the Animal Rescue Center now, and the ride would soon be over.

"But what could we do?" he asked Rafael.

"I'm sure you would figure it out," Rafael said. "I guess you could begin by investigating the rumors and where they come from and what they're about. Maybe someone *is* doing some smuggling — even if it isn't Dr. Stonebridge."

"Geez," said Pete. "First capybaras and now antiquities. What *is* it about Santa Barbara?"

That made Rafael smile — though he also looked thoughtful, as if he was wondering what the answer to that question actually was.

Then he was pulling into the parking lot at the Rescue Center. It had been a while since Pete had been there, and he was glad to be back. Over the last year he'd watched as injured animals were rehabilitated, and abandoned baby animals were nursed until they were big enough to fend for themselves in the wild. The building wasn't much to look at – it was an old converted barn – but a lot of good things happened inside it.

Rafael parked the truck, got out, and helped Pete take his bike out of the back. Heat waves radiated off the black asphalt of the parking lot.

"There's a lot more to tell you," he said, "but for the moment we're out of time. The thing is, Dr. Stonebridge is down here in Rocky Beach for a few days. He's giving a lecture and a two-day workshop at Reedmore College."

"Really?" Pete said. Reedmore was where Bob Andrews's mother taught evolutionary biology and The Three Investigators' friend Phillipa Paxton taught history.

"I'm having dinner with him tonight," Rafael said. "I've been thinking that it's time to tell him what people are saying about him behind his back. If you give me the go-ahead, I'll suggest to him that it would be a good idea if The Three Investigators looked into the matter.

"People are always underestimating the four of you," he added, "and since you're so young, nobody would think anything of the fact that you were asking questions and looking around. And I know how good you are at investigating, so I think you'd quickly figure out what was going on. Maybe he has an enemy he doesn't even know he has who's trying to ruin him."

"Gee," Pete said. "It sounds pretty challenging," – though secretly he thought it would be great if they got up to Santa Barbara again and could see more of Rafael and his girlfriend Elena.

"I'm glad you're having a meeting later," Rafael said. "Will you talk to the others and see what they think? If you decide you want to take the case, maybe you could come over to Isabella's house tomorrow and meet with her and Wally and me and Dr. Stonebridge."

"I'll definitely talk it up," Pete said. "I bet I can persuade the others."

"I bet you can. See you soon," Rafael said. He climbed back in his truck, waved, and took off down the road, backfiring once or twice.

Wow! Pete thought. That had been unexpected! He'd been looking forward to learning what Bob had come up with, and now here he was with a case that had been brought to him by Rafael Solares! He felt excited and unsettled and eager to tell the others.

That morning Pete had gotten a call from Mr. Munson, his supervisor, asking if he'd come in for a few hours. Someone had found an abandoned litter of fox kits, and he needed help settling them in. As Pete walked into the center and into the main office, Mr. Munson thanked him for coming.

"Are you kidding me?" Pete said. "Where are the baby foxes?"

Still, even while he was getting to know them, Pete's mind kept wandering to what he'd talked about with Rafael, and time seemed to move more slowly than usual. He cleaned out a few cages and then asked Mr. Munson if he needed any more help. When he told Pete to go, he practically ran out of the center and jumped onto his bike.

It was the hottest part of the day, but Pete didn't care. He rode as fast as he could to the Salvage Yard. He expected to see Jupiter, Bob, and Mallory in the outside workshop, but when they weren't there, he knew they were inside the old mobile home that The Three Investigators had been calling Headquarters since Jupiter had founded the firm several years before.

It was dark in there, and cluttered, and

Pete was glad to remember that Jupiter had asked Mallory to design a new Headquarters – or at least an office where they could have meetings, and even meet clients, and which they'd build the following spring.

For now, they were stuck with Headquarters as the only place they could have privacy for their case consultations, and since all of the other secret entrances had grown too small for The Three Investigators (as they'd grown larger), he went through Easy Three – the main entrance – and burst in.

Jupiter was sitting behind the desk in the swivel chair he always chose, and Mallory and Bob were sitting in chairs looking at him. Bob had a portfolio on his lap and a manila folder that Pete assumed held the e-mail inquiries he'd gotten.

"Hi, guys!" Pete said. He was overheated, sweating, and a bit out of breath, but very excited.

"Pete," Jupiter said. "You're just in time. Bob was about to start telling us about the inquiries he's gotten."

"That's just it!" Pete said. "I've already got us a new case. You won't believe who I ran into on my way to the Rescue Center. Rafael Solares! He wants us to help a friend of his – a

Classics professor at UC Santa Barbara – who people think is smuggling antiquities out of Greece, but who Rafael is certain isn't doing that at all!"

What a relief to finally say it! Pete thought. The tension had been building in his chest ever since Rafael had driven out of the Center's parking lot. Even better was the look of surprise on his friends' faces!

2

Godwin Cuthbert Stonebridge

The silence following Pete's announcement was deafening. Though Bob was always glad to see his friend, he was both startled by Pete's sudden appearance and a bit annoyed by the unexpected news. He, Jupiter, and Mallory had been sitting patiently waiting for Pete to show up so that Bob could get started with his presentation. Now the muscles of his face tightened and he opened his mouth to speak and then quickly closed it, unable to keep from showing how he felt.

Pete saw his expression. "What?" he asked.

"Nothing," Bob said, looking down at the papers in his lap. At Jupiter's suggestion, he'd spent the morning in his role as Records and Research printing out and going over the inquiries he'd received at The Three Investigators' e-mail address. Unfortunately, they were mostly the same inquiries he'd found uninteresting a week or more before – when he'd ended up urging the team to pursue what might have been a wild goose chase in the

Napa Valley. Luckily, that had panned out nicely.

When Bob had first started writing up The Three Investigators' cases and posting them online, he'd imagined that the people who read the reports would be their next eager clients, but it hadn't worked out that way at all, and when Pete burst into Headquarters with his news about Rafael Solares, Bob knew at once that he'd wasted his morning again.

"Rafael Solares!" Jupiter said. "What's he doing in Rocky Beach?"

"He came down to visit some old friends from high school," Pete said, grabbing a chair and settling in. "He's staying with Wally and Isabella, but if he hadn't run into me on the road – well, not run into, of course! – he said he'd planned to come by the Salvage Yard, anyway."

"How is he?" Mallory asked. She was sitting a bit back from the group around the desk and had been drawing lines on a pad of graph paper. Maybe she was working on a possible design for the new Three Investigators Headquarters, Bob thought.

"He's great!" Pete said.

"This is a surprise," Jupiter said to Pete. "You'd better gather your thoughts and tell us all about it."

Bob, too, was interested to hear Pete's news, but he decided to see if his acting skills were any better than they'd been the last time he'd tried them out. Though Jupiter and Mallory both had a talent for acting, Bob knew he was terrible at it. If he even tried to tell a simple fib, his eyes took on a certain deer-in-the-headlights quality, which gave him away immediately.

Still, pretending he was disappointed at not sharing the work he'd done should be easy – at least compared to something that would be hard! So he cleared his throat.

"But Jupe, you wanted to hear about the inquiries we'd gotten," he said, trying to make his voice sound a little miffed.

"That's true. I did," Jupiter said.

"Well," Bob said, "I think it would be a good idea to keep in mind all the possibilities. Why don't I just tell you about the inquiries I think are most interesting, and then Pete can tell us about Rafael?"

"That would be fine," Jupiter said. "Pete, you don't mind waiting, do you?"

From the expression on Pete's face, Bob could see he minded quite a lot. In fact, he looked like he might explode. Although he was now planted on a chair, he couldn't sit still for an instant.

Bob almost took pity on him, but when Pete said, "Come on! Let's hear the best ones!" he picked up several of the papers on his lap and carefully put them back in the zippered black portfolio he used for Three Investigators business.

"Those might turn into something," he said, as sadly as he could manage, "but I think I should just read these." He picked up the remaining pages. "I don't know which one you guys might like the best."

"Just choose one!" Pete said. "Hurry up! Rafael's friend needs our help!"

Jupiter held up his hand. "Let's let Bob finish," he said.

Pete stopped jiggling and sat back in resignation.

"Here's one," Bob said, trying to act enthusiastic about what he was reading. He doubted he was being successful.

"It's from a man in Castroville. He says his father never had a bank account and so he guesses that he must have kept all his money in gold. He says it has to be buried somewhere on his family's artichoke farm and that maybe we can find it."

"How big is the farm?" Pete asked, slightly interested. Bob knew Pete was a sucker for cases involving hidden treasure.

"A thousand acres," Bob said, with as straight a face as possible.

All four of them started laughing.

"Next!" said Mallory.

The Three Investigators had met Mallory the summer before when she'd moved with her mother to Rocky Beach from Scotland after her Scottish father had died. Early in the summer she'd biked by the Jones Salvage Yard and had stopped because of a stunt involving a battered suit of armor cooked up by Jupiter's Uncle Titus. Pete had started talking to her, and about a week later, through a happy accident, she'd been in northern California at the same time they'd been there on their first case of the summer. Since then, she'd made herself indispensable to their investigations.

With her shoulder-length red hair, her serious attitude, and her piercing intelligence, Mallory had been a great addition to their detective firm, and since she and Bob were not just friends but also climbing partners, it made Bob uncomfortable to see her looking at him skeptically.

With less and less enthusiasm, he read

two other letters from people who clearly had fixated on their case from the previous summer during which they'd uncovered a bag of gold nuggets hidden for over a hundred years – the case on which they'd met Mallory.

"Our discovery of Li Chang's gold certainly seems to have had a large effect on the imaginations of a certain part of our potential client base," Jupiter observed.

"You can say that again!" Pete said. "As well as a large effect on us! If we hadn't gone looking for information about Isabella Chang's ancestor, we might never have gotten to buy our own car. Or met Mallory!"

Mallory grinned wickedly from behind her pad of graph paper. "From the order in which you mentioned them, I can see which one was more important to you," she said.

Bob knew she was only kidding, but Pete instantly blushed. He blushed often and easily, and Bob had long felt sorry for him about it.

"That's not what I meant!" Pete said.

"I was only kidding," Mallory said. "Boy, do you turn red."

"I know!" Pete said. "I can't help it! It's like a curse."

Pete's discomfort made Bob feel badly about having teased him.

"Anyway, Pete, I was kidding, too – about the cases," Bob said. "I'm sure that whatever Rafael wants us to do will be a *lot* more interesting than anything I've got here. Go ahead and tell us all about it."

Pete took a deep breath and erupted in a torrent of words. As Pete told them what Rafael had said, Bob found himself becoming more and more interested. For one thing, he found the idea of an archaeologist fascinating – even an absent-minded one who didn't know people were talking behind his back.

Also, Bob was a history buff, and though he knew something about ancient Greece, his knowledge wasn't great. It would be fun to learn some more. That was, if Rafael managed to persuade this Dr. Stonebridge that The Three Investigators were the proper people to look into the rumors about him.

"I hate rumors and gossip," Mallory said. "They're almost always malicious."

"Yes, indeed," Jupiter said, "and difficult to diffuse or fight. If we take this case, we will have to engage ourselves in the mystery of why someone would propagate falsehoods about this man."

"We might as well find out as much about this Dr. Stonebridge as we can," Bob said. "Time to do some research."

He pulled his chair as close to the battered desk as he could, turned the old desktop computer toward him, and booted it up.

"What did you say his name was again?" he asked Pete.

"Dr. Stonebridge," Pete said.

"His whole name," Bob said patiently.

"His first name is Godwin," Pete said. "Is that enough? I can't remember his middle name. Something like Cutthroat."

Pete, Mallory, and Jupiter came to stand behind him as Bob searched UC Santa Barbara's website. He clicked on the Classics Department. From there he clicked on a listing of the department's faculty members. He scrolled down. There weren't that many of them, but at the bottom of the list was Dr. G. C. Stonebridge.

Bob stared at the photo next to his name. In it, Dr. Stonebridge was standing on a rock with the bright blue sky and dark ocean behind him. The sun was fierce and he cast a black shadow. The man was squinting, which scrunched up his face. He was wearing khaki shorts and a long-sleeved cambric shirt, boots that had seen a lot of hard use, and red socks that came halfway up his very white legs. On his head was a sort of safari hat.

Bob thought Dr. Stonebridge looked very intense but also very innocent – as though he lived in the realm of ideas and not in a world where rumors could ruin a person's reputation.

Looking away from the picture, Bob began to read his biography aloud.

"It says that Dr. Stonebridge was born in Liverpool, England, went to something called a grammar school, and then attended Cambridge University where he stayed on to get his Ph.D. He teaches one semester each year in Santa Barbara and spends the other half of the year in Greece, working on archaeological digs."

Bob clicked on a link to another page. "Here's a list of his publications," he said. He started scrolling down. "It's long. Really long."

"Wow!" Pete said. "He's a serious dude! Though he looks like a serious nerd."

Mallory laughed. "He looks like a typical university professor," she said, "if you want my opinion."

"We know plenty of university professors who don't look like that," Pete said, a little defensively. "Phillipa Paxton doesn't and neither does Bob's mother. He looks like the kind of guy who's never had a girlfriend."

"I agree, Bob said. "I mean, he doesn't look like a guy who puts a lot of emphasis on relationships. Though he must at least have some friends, or Rafael wouldn't be worried about him."

"Perhaps he'll look different in person – if he decides he wants to meet us," Jupiter said. "Besides, if he really is the victim of vicious and unfounded rumors – rumors he may not even know about yet – his looks may suit his personality. See if there's anything else you can find, Bob."

Bob went back to the page listing the Classics faculty at UC Santa Barbara. He glanced at several of the other professors who looked much younger and more hip than Dr. Stonebridge – but who were also much less accomplished, well-published, or imposing. Each of them had a dedicated website. But not Dr. Stonebridge.

"That doesn't surprise me," Jupiter said. "He doesn't look like the type who would be into self-advertisement or self-promotion."

"He doesn't look like the type who'd know how to put together a website," Pete said. "He looks like the pen and pencil type."

Bob typed "G. C. Stonebridge archaeology" into the browser's search box and pressed Enter. In no time, he'd uncovered a list of other sites with information about Dr. Stonebridge.

"His middle name, as it turns out," Bob said, "is Cuthbert, not Cutthroat, Pete."

"I got the first part right!" Pete said.

"And here's a longer bio on Archaeology.com," Bob said. He read it to himself, then shared the information with his friends. "It says that he's a Fellow of the British Academy and of the Society of Antiquaries, and his first important archaeological work took place on the Greek island of Naxos – . Wait! That's where Chris Markos said in his e-mail he's living now!"

"Chris lives on the island of Naxos?" Pete asked excitedly. "That's totally amazing! Rafael has another friend from Naxos, too – a rich business guy named Dimitri something."

This really *was* amazing, Bob thought. What a coincidence about Chris Marxos. If this case really turned into something – which by now Bob was certain it would – it might prove very helpful to have a friend in Greece.

Though Bob thought of saying this aloud, instead he just keep reading.

"It says here that after he worked on

Naxos, Dr. Stonebridge found some important artifacts on a very small uninhabited island not far from there. Then he moved on to the island of Crete where he was one of three archaeologists who discovered something called the Minoan Treasure. Look at the pictures!" he added.

These showed an amazing collection of gold objects − mostly jewelry − and as Bob and the others pointed, and counted, they could see that it included five pairs of earrings, each pair more elaborate than the next, with representations of snakes and owls and the heads of what looked to be bulls.

As well, there were chokers and necklaces made of strings of gold beads decorated with other precious stones, gold ornaments meant to be worn on strings around the neck, bracelets of thick gold that seemed to whirl around imaginary wrists, and beautiful engraved gold goblets and cups.

Because of the style of the pieces, Dr. Stonebridge and his fellow archaeologists had determined that they'd been crafted during the Greek Bronze Age − the three hundred years ranging from 1850 to 1550 B.C.E.

Bob was able to click on each of the pictures and then enlarge it, so that all four of them could see clearly how beautiful the individual pieces were.

"Wow!" Pete said. "Talk about buried treasure! Can you imagine what it was like to discover these, just lying in the dirt, buried for all those years? Now I understand why someone might want to be an archaeologist!"

"They *are* very beautiful," Mallory said. "And it must have been incredibly exciting to brush the dirt carefully off each one of them and see what lay underneath it. Still, I bet that good archaeologists are excited to find anything at all. It must be like traveling back in time."

But although, in a way, Bob agreed with that, it still seemed to him that each of the pieces was more astounding than the one before it. The gold was luminous. Some of it had been poured into molds as molten gold – particularly the gold beads that adorned several necklaces – and some of it was hand-hammered and remarkably thin. Some of it was engraved. Several of the rings and pendants were inlayed with the beautiful bright red of cornelian and the subtle jade of lapis lazuli.

Dr. Stonebridge and the others had found a number of smaller objects along with the major pieces. There were beads made of quartz and amethyst, gold rings, and many small gold objects that looked like buttons. It was an amazing find and was now in a museum in Athens.

Bob read that what was now known as the Minoan Treasure was very much like another discovery known as the Aegina Treasure – a horde of mostly gold objects found in a tomb during the late 19th century on the island of Aegina. But Dr. Stonebridge's hoard was larger and more significant, it seemed.

Just then, Bob and the others were startled when the landline in Headquarters rang. They used it so rarely and received so few calls on it that most of the time they more or less forgot it was even there.

Since Bob was sitting in front of the computer, in the swivel chair, Jupiter hurried back around the desk, punched the speakerphone button, and said, "Three Investigators Headquarters. Jupiter Jones speaking."

The voice that came over the phone was so familiar, Bob would have known who it was even if he hadn't identified himself. Just last year, he'd heard the voice for the first time when his cellphone had rung.

"Jupiter!" Rafael Solares said. "It's me! Rafael! I expect Pete's there by now and has told you we ran into each other earlier."

"I'm here!" Pete said cheerfully. Both Bob and Mallory chimed in with "Hi, Rafael!"

"Hello," Jupiter said. "It's good to hear your voice. Yes, we're all here, and we're eager to hear more about this potential case. From what Pete told us, so far this is just your idea, and the possible client doesn't know anything about it."

"That's correct," Rafael said. "As I'm sure Pete has already told you, I'm having dinner with Dr. Stonebridge this evening. But before I ask him anything, I wanted to know if you four are interested in investigating the rumors."

"We'd want to know we had his approval first," Jupiter said.

"Of course," Rafael said. "But I think I can persuade him to give you that."

"Then, we certainly would be interested," Jupiter said.

"I was hoping you'd say that," Rafael said. "If Dr. Stonebridge is on board with the idea, we can all meet at Wally and Isabella's tomorrow. I'm sure Pete told you I'm staying with them. In fact, that's where I'm calling from. Both of them would love to see all of you, and I just learned that many years ago

Isabella traveled to Greece. She's anxious to meet an archaeologist like Dr. Stonebridge who's worked there."

Bob thought that meeting Dr. Stonebridge at Isabella Chang's was a great idea. Ever since he'd met Isabella during the first case of the previous summer, he'd had a special liking for her. Before she'd retired, she'd taught history, and Bob was also very interested in history. Aside from that, he was impressed with her calmness, her wisdom, and her generosity and kindness.

And Wally Tate was one of Bob's favorite people. He'd lived for more than ninety years, had fought in World War II, and knew a lot about literature — which was what *he'd* taught before he retired. On top of all that, Wally was one of the wittiest people Bob had ever met. During the school year, Bob had made a point of staying in touch with them and visiting when he could. But he hadn't seen them since school let out.

"Let us know how your talk with Dr. Stonebridge goes," Jupiter said.

"I will," Rafael said. "But I have the feeling it will go well, so unless I call you back to say it won't work after all, why don't we plan on eleven o'clock tomorrow, at Isabella's? Can you all make it?"

Bob watched as Jupiter took a quick inventory of everyone nodding.

"We'll be there," Jupiter said. Everyone said goodbye, and Jupiter hung up − at which point Bob finally got to say what he had been about to say to the others before Rafael called.

"I think it's interesting that Dr. Stonebridge started his career on Naxos, and amazing that we suddenly know someone who lives there," he said. "Who knows where this case will lead us, but if we need him, I'm sure Chris would do whatever he could to help. He wants to Skype, and he sent us his number and Skype handle. He could be our eyes and ears on the ground if we need that. Now all I have to do is figure out how to use Skype to call out of the country. It can't be that hard. After all, I've already used it to talk to Hector Sebastian in Wyoming. I'll just have to remember the time difference."

"What is it?" Pete asked.

"When I got Chris's e-mail, I looked it up," Bob answered. "Naxos is ten hours ahead of us. When it's noon here, it's ten at night on Naxos."

"That's going to make it hard," Pete said.

"Yes," Jupiter said, "but not impossible."

"No, not impossible!" said Bob. Suddenly, he felt terrific. The slight grumpiness he'd felt when Pete had arrived was totally gone. The new case sounded far more interesting than any of the e-mail inquiries he'd gotten. So what if none of them ever turned into a case? The important thing was that The Three Investigators continued to find cases that intrigued and challenged them, and this new case looked like it would fit the bill.

Of course Dr. Stonebridge would say yes to getting them involved in it! Who could say no to Rafael Solares? Bob thought.

3

A Plan To Run Down Rumors

Jupiter slept late the following morning and woke with a start to see that it was already 9:00 and that he had only two hours to get up, take a shower, get dressed, eat breakfast, and prepare his thoughts for the meeting with Dr. Stonebridge. As he woke, he suddenly remembered that, at some point while he had slept, he had dreamed he was living in ancient Greece and taking part in one of the original Olympic games as a contestant.

In his dream, the landscape around him and his fellow sportsmen was bare and sere and shimmering with the same kind of dry heat California sometimes had, and he and another fencer had been parrying – even though Jupiter knew from his fencing coach that Jupiter's chosen sport hadn't become an Olympic event until 1896. The ancient Greeks who had lived near and in Olympia had held foot races and jumping contests, had thrown javelins and discuses, and had also had wrestling and boxing matches, but although they had undoubtedly also practiced a form of fencing, they hadn't made it into an Olympic sport.

Still, in his dream, it hadn't seemed strange at all to be wearing modern fencing kit and thrusting with a modern foil. For the whole of the past year, Jupiter had been part of the very small fencing team at Rocky Beach High, and since the school year had come to an end, he'd missed his practice sessions and the knowledge that he was improving all the time. Fencing was the first sport he'd ever actually been good at, and as he got up, showered, dressed, then went to the kitchen for some cereal, he kept thinking about his dream, and about ancient Greece.

He had to admit he was pretty ignorant about what had gone on there and might actually have imagined that the ancient Games had featured fencing if his coach hadn't told him otherwise. But although he grabbed a book about Greece and Rome from the bookcase where it had been sitting, unread, for several years now, he didn't really have time to read any of it before the others were arriving, on their bikes.

Soon, they were all starting off together for Isabella's house. There – after they'd taken off their helmets and stowed their bikes – Pete rang the doorbell and Jupiter, Bob, and Mallory stood behind him on the flagstone walk. Usually, when they visited, Wally answered the door — quick with a smile and a witty comment — so Jupiter was surprised when the door opened and Rafael Solares stood there.

He looked just as he had when they'd met him the previous summer — lean and tan and radiating peacefulness, his fine long black hair pulled back into a ponytail — but another man stood behind him in the house's foyer.

Though he was in shadow, Jupiter could see that it must be Dr. Stonebridge, looking quite different than he had on the UC Santa Barbara website. For one thing, in the photo he'd been dwarfed by the landscape he appeared in — all that sky and sea — and here there was nothing to distract Jupiter from the gravity of his demeanor and the calmness of his presence.

He was wearing a dark blue jacket, a subdued red tie, and charcoal gray slacks. His brown Oxfords were highly polished. Though he wasn't quite as tall as Rafael, he was tall — somewhere over six feet — and quite slender, although his hands and wrists and feet were big. They looked slightly out of proportion to the rest of his body.

Jupiter noticed the wrists in particular

because a glint of silver had caught his attention. On his left wrist Dr. Stonebridge wore an expensive-looking watch, and on his right wrist a simple cuff of silver that struck Jupiter as a little bit odd. Men like Dr. Stonebridge might wear a wedding ring – Jupiter could see that Dr. Stonebridge's fingers were quite bare – but beyond that, a piece of jewelry like a silver bracelet was unusual.

All this Jupiter observed in a flash, because as soon as the door had opened, Rafael was welcoming them in and introducing them one by one to Dr. Stonebridge, who shook their hands and looked earnestly into their eyes. Jupiter was struck by how mild Dr. Stonebridge's gaze was. He was clearly not someone who went around looking for a fight.

"I'm pleased to meet you all," Dr. Stonebridge said in the rich deep British accent Jupiter associated with costume dramas on public television. "However, I'm a bit confused. Rafael told me that you were called The Three Investigators, but if my mathematical skills haven't completely deserted me, there are four of you."

"You've counted correctly," Jupiter said. "Pete, Bob, and I are The Three Investigators. Mallory is a Special Consultant to our firm.

We've found her help invaluable."

Dr. Stonebridge turned to Mallory. "Are you from Scotland, my dear?" he asked.

Jupiter was so used to Mallory's accent by this time that he found himself surprised by the question. Now that he focused on it, he realized that she *did* sound Scottish, and probably always would.

"In a way," Mallory said, explaining that she'd grown up in Scotland and then had moved to America after the death of her father. As Jupiter listened to her tell the story, he was impressed, as he always was, with her poise. But as he watched Dr. Stonebridge listen attentively and nod sympathetically, Jupiter was also impressed with his.

"Wally and Isabella are waiting in the back by the koi pond, as you will have expected," Rafael said. "Why don't we join them?"

Rafael led the way, followed by Dr. Stonebridge, and then the four of them in single file. It was quite a procession, Jupiter thought.

They walked down the hall and into the spare living room where the birdcage hung with the two lovebirds Pete had given to Wally and Isabella at the end of the animal smuggling case. Then they went out the glass doors into Isabella's backyard.

As Rafael had said, Wally and Isabella were sitting in chairs around the metal outdoor table that had been set in the shade by the koi pond, where golden fish surfaced from time to time as if to take a look at the wider world.

"Hello, you four," Wally said. "Welcome!"

"Yes," Isabella said. "It's always such a pleasure to see you. Come, sit. As you can see there's a pitcher of lemonade and a plate of cookies. You must help yourselves."

"Thanks," Pete said, grabbing a cookie before grabbing a seat. Jupiter smiled. Pete could always be counted on to appreciate Isabella's hospitality.

"I do not think there have been so many distinguished personages in one place," Wally said, "since Thomas Jefferson dined alone."

He raised his eyebrows and smiled slyly, which made Isabella laugh.

"I know, I know," Wally went on, nodding and waving his hand in the air as if to quell objections. "That is not the correct quote, and this isn't the White House. Still, I am thrilled to see so many old friends."

Jupiter enjoyed Wally's often barbed,

ironic wit and was waiting for the zinger, but it never came. It seemed that today, Wally was simply glad to see everybody.

"Rafael has done us the honor of introducing us to this esteemed archaeologist," Wally said to Jupiter and the others. He turned to Dr. Stonebridge. "Though I was not previously familiar with your work, I'm happy to say that Isabella — who exceeds me in all things — was. She has long had an interest in Greek history and culture. In fact, we neglected to mention before that she's been to Naxos."

"Have you, my dear?" Dr. Stonebridge said, turning to Isabella.

She nodded. "Thirty years ago now," she said. "I'm sure everything has changed a great deal."

"That is certainly so," Dr. Stonebridge said, "and not always for the better." Dr. Stonebridge folded his hands together and rested them on the table. As he did, Jupiter got a better look at the bracelet on his right wrist. It was about a half inch wide, though it flared at both ends and also in the middle where some Greek letters had been stamped. On either end were common geometric designs.

"Pardon my interruption," Jupiter said, "but that's a very interesting bracelet. Could I ask what those stamped letters are?"

"This?" Dr. Stonebridge asked, surprised. He made an attempt to shoot his cuff, to cover the bracelet. "Those are my initials in Greek. Gamma for Godwin, Sigma for Stonebridge," he said. "Do you know the Greek alphabet?"

"No," Jupiter said, shaking his head.

"You should learn it," Dr. Stonebridge said – his voice a little prickly, Jupiter thought.

"Godwin," Rafael murmured. Dr. Stonebridge swiveled to face his friend. "Excuse me for getting right to the point, but I did want you to talk to my young friends about the problem facing you."

An amused expression flashed across Dr. Stonebridge's face, as though he understood Rafael's intentions were good but that he was making too much of a fuss.

"As I told you," he said, "I cannot take these rumors seriously. People will talk about the strangest things, and I've always thought it was best to ignore them."

"That may be so, Dr. Stonebridge," Jupiter said. "But a small fire can get out of control if it is not quickly extinguished."

Dr. Stonebridge looked impressed by Jupiter's analogy. "That is a wise observation for someone so young," he said.

Jupiter chose that moment to pull from his wallet one of The Three Investigators' business cards he carried with him at all times and handed it to Dr. Stonebridge. The professor studied it.

"This is very professional," he said. "And a chimera! Very clever! I presume it stands for you three boys?"

Pete, whose idea the chimera had been, beamed.

"That's correct," Jupiter said.

Dr. Stonebridge smiled. "But even with the combined power of three such extraordinary animals, what do you think you – or anyone – can do about these rumors? What do people do on college campuses? They talk. Rumors are always swirling around the Santa Barbara campus, each more ridiculous than the last. They're like silly little viruses that run their course and die out when everyone loses interest."

"I hope that's the case with these," Jupiter said. "But I do think it would be prudent to look into them. After all, Rafael has heard them from three different people he works with – people he presumably has a good opinion of."

"That's right," Rafael said.

Dr. Stonebridge nodded thoughtfully. "I guess there can be no harm in you doing a little investigating. How would you start, though?"

"By interviewing you," Jupiter said, "to see if we can uncover anything that would give us a lead."

"Ask away!" Dr. Stonebridge said.

Jupiter got to work. He sat forward and stared at Dr. Stonebridge intently. How long had he been teaching at Santa Barbara? he asked. Did he have any adversaries among his colleagues? Any students who might have a grudge? Any professional rivals? Any enemies?

No, Dr. Stonebridge told him. None that he knew of.

Was he married, Jupiter asked, or had he been? Did he have any children?

Though Dr. Stonebridge seemed taken aback by these last two questions, he told Jupiter he had never been married and had no children.

Remembering Pete's observation, Jupiter then asked if Dr. Stonebridge was in a relationship.

At this question, Dr. Stonebridge seemed actively embarrassed – but responded with a dismissive laugh and a long series of nos, as if nothing could be more ridiculous.

Jupiter could see that his first line of questioning was a failure and decided to change the subject.

"If I may ask," he said, "what exactly are you doing this summer?"

At this question, Dr. Stonebridge suddenly looked animated and happy.

"Aside from the small teaching opportunity down here in Rocky Beach, I'm involved in an unusual and exciting project," he replied. "My great friend Dimitri Dimitriou and I have been working for months to arrange, curate, and open a major exhibit at the Santa Barbara Museum of Antiquities, where I am an official advisor. We've been able to get Athens to loan us the Bronze Age hoard I and several other archaeologists discovered on Crete about twenty years ago."

"You mean the Minoan Treasure?" Bob asked excitedly.

"You've been researching me!" Dr. Stonebridge said, clearly pleased. "Yes, exactly. The Minoan Treasure, as it's called. It's never left Greece before. But Dimitri, who is Greek, and a great philanthropist – he helped to build and fund the Museum of Antiquities itself – was very persuasive. The exhibit has been a huge success ever since its opening earlier this month, and now so many more people know about our museum. We're really fortunate to be able to exhibit such a magnificent hoard."

"Wait a minute," Pete said. "I'm confused. I thought a horde was a big bunch of people, usually angry. Like the Mongol Horde."

Dr. Stonebridge laughed. "They're two different words, young man. You're right about *your* 'horde.' *My* hoard has an 'a' in it and is just another word for treasure trove."

"I haven't been up to Santa Barbara," Isabella said suddenly, "and I'm sure the exhibit is spectacular. But as impressive as gold treasure can be, what I always loved about the Greek classical period were the large bronze sculptures – like the one of Poseidon in the National Archaeological Museum in Athens."

"It's interesting that you should mention that astounding statue," Dr. Stonebridge said. "Archaeologists are now uncertain as to whether the statue depicts Poseidon or Zeus. Whatever he was holding in his right hand is now lost. If it were a trident, that would indicate Poseidon; if it were a lightning bolt that would indicate Zeus. Because of the position of the arm, most archaeologists now favor Zeus."

"How fascinating," Isabella said. "Of course, I saw the statue thirty years ago – though time had little meaning for me when I was in the Cyclades. With the blue sky and the endless sea and the whitewashed buildings, it could have been any time at all. When I was there, the rule of the Greek military junta had ended and life was more relaxed again."

"The military junta?" Jupiter asked.

"For seven years – from 1967 until 1974 – Greece was ruled by a group of Greek generals," Isabella said. "They would sit around in cafés in Athens, wearing side arms and intimidating the people. Very repressive."

"It was a nasty period," Dr. Stonebridge said. "I always thought it curious that during the time the military ruled Greece, the Ministry of Culture and Science was founded. It seemed counterintuitive."

"That's an odd combination," Mallory said. "Culture and science."

Dr. Stonebridge explained that the ministry had changed its name frequently over the years and now was called the Ministry of Culture and Sports – in charge of all of Greece's museums and all its archaeological sites, but also in charge of promoting the arts and overseeing sports. But from its founding it had always been in charge of Greece's antiquities. Like all government agencies, there were good and bad things about it, and good and bad people who worked for it, Dr. Stonebridge said.

"I've never personally had a problem with the Ministry," Dr. Stonebridge said. "But many Greeks resent it. The Ministry asserts control over all the archaeological sites in the country, including all the undiscovered sites. And I cannot begin to tell you how many there are. You can barely kick a bit of dirt in Greece without unearthing some ancient coins – if not something a good deal more valuable and important."

"Really?" Bob said.

"Yes, indeed," Dr. Stonebridge said. "The country is one vast archaeological site."

"I'd like to go to Greece," Pete said, "and find something cool! Maybe something worth a lot!"

"Whether it was worth a lot or a little," Dr. Stonebridge said, "you'd have to give it to the Greek government."

"Why?" Pete said indignantly. "That doesn't seem fair. "Finders keepers."

"That may be true in the United States," Dr. Stonebridge said, "but not in Greece. The law clearly states that all antiquities are the property of the government. That's what I meant about ordinary Greeks resenting the Ministry of Culture and Sport. Ever since Greece began using the euro as its unit of currency, the country has been in economic turmoil, and a lot of ordinary people are desperately poor."

"Before the euro, Greece used the drachma, I believe," Jupiter remarked.

This was something else he'd remembered on the bike ride over to Isabella's house, but like many things he knew, he had no idea exactly how he knew it. Perhaps he'd heard a teacher – or a newscaster – mention it.

"Indeed," Dr. Stonebridge said. "The modern drachma was replaced by the euro in 2002. The drachma has been used in Greece through much of its history – starting with any number of city states like Athens and Sparta. The silver tetradrachm was also used during the Hellenistic period. The modern drachma was issued in 1832, I believe."

"What's the Hellenistic period?" Pete asked.

"The era of Greek history that begins with the death of Alexander the Great – a time when Greek objects, culture, and values were spreading around the world," Dr. Stonebridge said. "And as culture spread, so too did the drachma. Especially the tetradrachm with the head of Alexander on it. You can find them almost anywhere in Greece. In the fifth century B.C.E. it was a lot was a lot of money – a skilled laborer's pay for four days of work.

"But today, because of the laws concerning antiquities, anyone who finds one and keeps it is a criminal. The law seems designed to turn ordinary people into lawbreakers."

"So it's not like that everywhere?" asked Pete.

"Absolutely not," Dr. Stonebridge said. "For example, back in Great Britain – Mallory, you probably already know this – if you find buried treasure, it belongs partly to you, partly to the person whose land it was discovered on, and partly to the Crown. That seems much more fair."

"Back in Scotland," Mallory said, "I had a friend who found a gold coin, and with the money he got, he bought a metal detector and found five more!"

"Good for him," Dr. Stonebridge said. "But in Greece, it all belongs to the government. It's a bad situation, really."

"And a very sad situation," Isabella said,

"from what I've been able to learn from news-papers and magazines. Over the last few years the unemployment rate in Greece has hovered near 20%. When I was there, though, everyone was working. Many people catered to tourists, but they grew olives and grapes, and there were plenty of other businesses, too."

"That's true," Dr. Stonebridge said. "The economy hadn't yet been destroyed. Though it's slowly getting better, people are still having a terrible time, even with all the tourists. If they find ancient silver drachmas, you can bet they're not giving them to the government. In fact, I wouldn't be surprised to learn that the rumors may have arisen from the twisted fact that poor Greeks are hunting for old coins and then selling them to smugglers who sneak them out of the country and sell them abroad."

"It's pretty ironic," Bob said thoughtfully, "that modern Greeks are selling ancient Greek money to non-Greeks, for the simple reason that modern Greek money is worth so little!"

"Quite ironic," Dr. Stonebridge said. "And it's not just ancient coins that are getting smuggled out of Greece. Other antiquities, too – much rarer, often one of a kind, some of them undoubtedly priceless – are being sold for next to nothing."

He sighed and shook his head. Jupiter could see he took this very personally.

"Of course, no archaeologist would ever participate in any such scheme," Dr. Stonebridge said. "People who traffic in stolen antiquities wind up erasing the archaeological record, and the history of a culture, and the whole point and joy of archaeology is to better understand the past and where we as a species came from.

"However," Dr. Stonebridge went on, "not everyone is an archaeologist, or sees it the way I see it. In every country with an ancient history, people smuggle antiquities, but in Greece the situation is especially tragic because modern Greek law refuses to recognize simple human nature. That's ironic, too, because one of the cornerstone values of ancient Greek culture was reciprocity."

"What does that mean?" Bob asked.

"Two or more people exchanging things for the benefit of all parties," Dr. Stonebridge said. "It relies on the good will and honor of all participants. But as you have heard, there is no honor among thieves — which is what the Greek government is forcing many of its citizens to be. Behaving honorably was an important value in ancient Greece — a value that Greece bequeathed to the world, but that hasn't always survived. To put it mildly. But my friend Dimitri Dimitriou still lives by that value. In fact, he is one of the most honorable men I have ever met, as well as being the single richest!"

Jupiter thought this was interesting and asked what he meant.

Dr. Stonebridge smiled. "Because he has been given so much by the world, Dimitri believes that it is his responsibility to give back in equal measure. So philanthropy is very important to him. Not only did he mostly fund the antiquities museum, he also helps raise money for Special Education and other worthy causes.

"But beyond giving money, he also gives of himself. He is amazingly loyal and kind to old friends and acquaintances – including people he knew when he was just a boy on Naxos. As a matter of fact, when a childhood friend of his lost his wife in a boating accident, Dimitri brought him over to manage his oceanside estate. Interestingly, the man used to work for the Ministry of Culture and Sport for many years before he came to California to work for Dimitri."

"An estate manager?" Wally said. "Isabella and I manage our estate quite well, all by ourselves."

"You'd have to see it to understand," Dr. Stonebridge said. "It's almost a museum of the gifts Greece gave the modern world. For example, Dimitri had a small artificial island built just offshore, with a lighthouse, accessible only by an arched stone bridge."

"Did the Greeks invent the lighthouse?" Jupiter asked curiously.

"Yes," said Dr. Stonebridge. "The world's first lighthouse was built late in the third century B.C.E. off Alexandria and was one of the seven wonders of the ancient world. Of course, it no longer exists, but archaeologists believe it was over three hundred feet high. Dimitri's lighthouse is much smaller, and uses a modern light system — not the bonfire that the Lighthouse of Alexandria used. Still, it's quite impressive. He runs the light in it once a week."

"Why not every night?" Pete asked.

"Dimitri doesn't think his neighbors would appreciate it," Dr. Stonebridge said. "He's a very thoughtful man. Aside from his friend who manages the estate, Dimitri has also hired the oldest son of a Naxian family to run his import-export business. Perhaps you've heard of Aegean Treasures?"

Jupiter shook his head. "I don't think so,"

he said.

"Anyway," Dr. Stonebridge went on. "With the economic situation in Greece, the man was very grateful for the opportunity."

"Mr. Dimitriou sounds like a great guy," Pete said. "At least, he's great to his friends."

"Exactly," Dr. Stonebridge said. "That is the point I am trying to make. Dimitri is honorable and ethical, and it's wholly because of him that the Ministry in Greece has allowed the Minoan Treasure to leave the country. You really should get up to Santa Barbara to see it."

"We'd like that very much," Jupiter said. Even though Dr. Stonebridge was not enthusiastic about their help in finding out the source of the rumors, Jupiter thought that if they were able to get up to Santa Barbara, they could investigate on their own.

"Then perhaps I'll see you again," Dr. Stonebridge said graciously. "I'm heading back up to Santa Barbara this afternoon."

"If you wanted to come up," Rafael said to Jupiter and the others, "you could visit me and Elena, and see the exhibit. I'm pretty sure I could arrange for you to stay in university dorm rooms connected to the Special Ed program I'm involved with. "

"That would be so cool!" Pete said enthusiastically. "It'd be great to stay in a college dormitory! Though I hope we can also see that island and that lighthouse!" Jupiter could see his face suddenly cloud. "I just remembered I promised Mr. Munson I'd come in to feed and check on the baby foxes tomorrow morning."

"That shouldn't be a problem," Jupiter said. "We couldn't leave until day after tomorrow, anyway. And Rafael might not be able to arrange for us to stay in the dorm rooms that quickly."

"Actually, I probably could," Rafael said. "The dorm is brand new, and since it's summer, it's still almost empty. Day after tomorrow will be fine, though."

"If Pete has to work," Jupiter said, "maybe tomorrow morning the rest of us can do a bit more research."

But Bob said, "I have to work, too. I promised Miss Bennett I'd put in some hours at the library in the morning. She wants help with the monthly newsletter."

"If Bob's going to be there anyway," Mallory said to Jupiter, "maybe you and I could meet at the library at 10:00. I'll bring my laptop. Bob can join us if he has a break."

"That's a great idea," Bob said. "But I

doubt I'll have the time. Still, if you bring your lunches, you could tell me what you've found out when we eat."

"O.K.," Jupiter said. "Let's do it. We'd better be going. It was a pleasure to meet you, Dr. Stonebridge."

The professor rose, looking a little flustered. "I hope I haven't talked too much," he said. "The pleasure was all mine."

Rafael followed them out to the driveway. "Godwin's very shy," he said, "and doesn't want to make a fuss. But I can tell he really likes you."

"I like him, too," said Jupiter. He said goodbye to Rafael and told him they'd undoubtedly see him soon. Then the four of them got back on their bikes and, as they did, Jupiter accidentally bumped into Mallory. She laughed and flashed him a friendly smile.

Although he couldn't remember having worked alone on research with Mallory before, Jupiter was pleased with the idea – more than he would have imagined beforehand. In fact, he found he was suddenly quite looking forward to it. A year before at this time, he had hardly even *met* Mallory, and now she seemed to him almost as much a part of The Three Investigators as he and Bob and Pete.

4

Heading For Santa Barbara

At 9:00 the next morning, as she waited for it to be time to leave for the library, Mallory found herself thinking approximately the same thing. Her mother had long ago left for work, and Mallory had eaten breakfast in the kitchen by herself, then made a lunch to take with her.

Now she sat on the porch of the Wessex House in one of the old-fashioned rocking chairs, her laptop on her lap. She had a half-hour before she needed to leave, so she let her eyes close and just rocked back and forth while the neighborhood's automatic sprinklers sent cooling, sweet-smelling mist into the air. They were programmed to work early every morning, before the day began to heat up, and Mallory had long ago gotten used to the fact that the sprinklers were the only reason lawns in southern California were even remotely green.

Today their mist – and the sun in the fronds of the palm trees – reminded her of a day the summer before when she had biked to the Jones Salvage Yard quite early. She and her mother had been away from town for a few

67

days, and while she was gone, she'd found that she missed working at the Salvage Yard, missed The Three Investigators, and even missed Rocky Beach. At the time, this had surprised her, but now, almost a year later, it didn't surprise her at all.

The day she was remembering, she'd gotten to the Salvage Yard before anyone else, and when she'd biked past the wooden fence surrounding it − a fence local artists had covered with colorful murals − she'd seen that the not-so-secret entrance the boys called Green Gate One had almost been ripped off its hinges. Then she'd discovered that Headquarters itself had been broken into, and when Jupiter had invited her inside, she'd been thrilled − though surprised at how shabby Headquarters was. She'd wondered how long it would have taken Jupiter to get around to asking her inside if it hadn't been for the break-in. Another year, probably, she thought.

Of course, at the time, she'd only been in Rocky Beach a few months, and she'd kept reminding her mother of the promise she'd made to take Mallory back to Scotland if Mallory didn't like it in California after two years. She hadn't told her mother yet, but now − just a year after they'd moved there − she already knew she wanted to stay.

It was a strange place in lots of ways – very crowded practically everywhere there weren't mountains, and with more than its fair share of hypocrites and phonies – but there was a lot of energy in the air and a true appreciation of new ideas and new people. It was also a genuine melting-pot of cultures from all over the world.

The Three Investigators' last case had introduced them to an interesting Portuguese Muslim family who were now Americans, and a duo of Italian stonemasons in the United States just for the summer, as well as a half-Italian half-Swedish and all-fake Franciscan monk.

And that case had hardly been unusual, Mallory thought. In just the cases she herself had been involved with, The Three Investigators had had to uncover the motives behind the actions of a German artist, a British-Indian theatrical director, a Mexican-American historian, and a number of other people with strong connections to other cultures – and now, it seemed they were about to plunge into the life of a British archeologist who spent half of each year in Greece, and who was friends with one of the most well-known philanthropists in the

United States.

The night before, when she'd gotten back to her apartment, she'd decided to see what she could discover about the man Dr. Stonebridge had talked about so warmly – the Greek entrepreneur and businessman Dimitri Dimitriou.

She'd discovered that not only was he rich and successful and that his line of specialty stores called Aegean Treasures was expanding rapidly, but that he was very well liked by the community around Santa Barbara for his generosity and kindness.

As Dr. Stonebridge had said, he'd provided most of the funding that had built the Santa Barbara Museum of Antiquities and had arranged for the loan of the collection of ancient Greek treasure that Dr. Stonebridge was currently so proud of.

She glanced at her watch and saw that she still had some time before she had to leave for the library. Not thinking about it much one way or the other, she took out her cellphone and hit the button for her friend Califia García-Williams – the only female friend she'd made since she'd moved to Rocky Beach.

Although Mallory and Califia were both in the same grade at Rocky Beach High, Mallory had actually met her on the set of a movie

Califia's father had been in the summer before. Pete's father had been the construction supervisor for *Bear Valley*, and Mallory's mother had worked in the costume department, and Califia had actually given Mallory a little background information about both Jupiter and Pete when she herself had just met them.

Her call to Califia went straight to voicemail, so Mallory left her a brief message explaining that she, Jupiter, Pete, and Bob would be taking off tomorrow for Santa Barbara. After that, she opened her laptop and typed "Santa Barbara Museum of Antiquities" into the search bar. The headline that popped up made Mallory gasp.

"THIEVES STEAL PRICELESS HOARD," said a banner in the Santa Barbara *Clarion*.

Someone had stolen the Minoan Treasure!

Mallory's heart started pounding – and just at that moment, the sprinklers turned off. As Mallory looked around her in shock and alarm, it seemed to her, quite irrationally, that the strength of her emotion had somehow alerted the computer system and shut down the sprinklers. Or was her sudden knowledge of the theft and the sprinklers' stopping related in some way she didn't understand?

She took a deep breath and shook off this bizarre idea, reminding herself that though the world was filled with events that the human mind interpreted as signs and symbols, most of the time it was simple coincidence. She returned to her laptop to read the article with avid interest.

It seemed that two thieves dressed as policemen had knocked on the door of the Santa Barbara Museum of Antiquities at two in the morning, saying that they'd been sent to investigate a report of a break-in. The museum's two night watchmen had let them in, then found themselves overpowered, handcuffed, marched off to the basement, and fastened to some pipes. The thieves had then gone back to the room where the Minoan treasure was displayed. They'd shattered the glass cases that held it and made off with all of it.

Mallory read that the treasure had a value in the many, many millions of dollars, but since it was irreplaceable, it was also priceless. Though the museum had closed-circuit television cameras, the thieves had put on face masks before the cameras had caught any of their movements, and as of now, there were no real clues as to who they were, or where they had taken the treasure.

Well, apparently there was *one* clue, but the police weren't revealing that at the moment.

Mallory was flabbergasted. Just wait until the boys heard about this! she thought. She thrust her laptop into her backpack, buckled on her helmet, and took off at top speed for the library. Though she was right on time − it was ten o'clock − she wasn't surprised to find Jupiter already there, sitting on the rock retaining wall by the library's entrance. She glided to a stop, shoved her bike into the bike rack, locked it, and joined him.

"Guess what happened last night?" she said.

Jupiter looked up alertly and said, "Tell me."

"I'd rather show you," Mallory said. She sat beside him on the wall, took out her laptop, flipped it open, and handed it to him. She'd left the article about the theft up on her browser, and as Jupiter read the headline, his eyes flared, and then he very intently and quickly read the article.

Mallory watched his face, hoping to see the same sense of disbelief she'd experienced, and although Jupiter was remarkably restrained, when he handed her laptop back to her, she could tell from his eyes that he was pleased that the case has just expanded from what it had been before into something a good deal bigger and more exciting.

"Shall we go inside?" she asked, sliding off the stone wall. "Is Bob here yet?"

"He's already working," Jupiter said.

The last time Mallory had done research in the Rocky Beach Library in relation to a Three Investigators case, she and Bob had been looking for information about the British actor Sir Iain Anthony, and they'd had quite a successful morning, sending links back and forth and discussing them.

She was looking forward to seeing what it would be like to work alone with Jupiter. As they entered the library, she saw Bob shelving books. She waved to him as she and Jupiter chose an empty table close to the back windows which overlooked the library's courtyard.

Since Jupiter didn't have a laptop – preferring to use the desktop computer in Headquarters, and to rely on Bob's laptop when they were out and about – this morning, it would be a different process, Mallory knew.

Jupiter pulled up a chair next to hers, but they hadn't even started when Bob came over.

"I've got to make this quick," Bob said,

looking over his shoulder to see where Miss Bennett was, "but I wanted to say hello."

"You're not going to believe this," said Mallory in a low voice, "but the Antiquities Museum in Santa Barbara was ransacked last night. The Minoan Treasure has been stolen."

Bob's eyes flew open in surprise. "You're kidding."

"Unfortunately, I'm not," said Mallory. "Look." She gestured toward the article which was still open on her laptop.

"Wow!" Bob said. "What are the odds? We just learned about the treasure the day before yesterday, and yesterday we were talking to one of the men who discovered it. I bet the Greek government isn't pleased at all."

"No," Jupiter said. "I would expect not."

Bob read the article quickly, then raised the question that was also on Mallory's mind.

"I wonder what the police are holding back," he said.

"It must be something that would identify the thieves," Jupiter said, "which they want to investigate thoroughly before it becomes public."

"Like what?" Bob asked. "Fingerprints?"

"Doubtful," Jupiter said. "I'm sure they were wearing gloves."

"They probably didn't leave a business card," Mallory said.

"Probably not," Jupiter said, "but some thieves have been that careless or dumb. I read about a guy who was arrested for drug possession. He was carrying a Zip-Lok bag on which he'd written 'Bag Full of Drugs.'"

Bob smiled. "I've got to get back to work, but I wanted to tell you I e-mailed Chris Markos yesterday and asked if we can Skype with him soon, and I just heard back that we can have a call early this afternoon – which will be night in Greece. Just a thought as you research – jot down any questions for Chris that you can think of. See you at lunch."

He darted back to reshelving books that the library's patrons had returned, and Mallory and Jupiter got down to business.

"The first thing we ought to do," Jupiter suggested, "is find out as much about the robbery as we can."

Mallory agreed and started following links and leads from one newspaper account to another. News of the theft had spread widely and some people were even commenting on it on a social media site called Chat.

"Look at this," Mallory said, as she clicked on a link on a Chat comment. It took her to an article in the Boston *Herald* from 1990. As she read, she turned to Jupiter.

"The robbery last night was a copycat!" she said. "The thieves used the game plan of two thieves who stole a bunch of paintings from a museum in Boston over thirty years ago!"

It seemed that the original thieves had posed as policemen, overpowered the security guards, and then handcuffed them to pipes in the basement before taking their sweet time to steal a good number of famous paintings.

The theft, it turned out, was very famous, and Mallory found any number of articles trying to reconstruct the crime.

"The paintings are still missing," Mallory reported to Jupiter. "Not a single one has been recovered. The Boston museum was quite hopeful that they'd be found; they're still hopeful. But so far, no luck."

"All right," Jupiter said. "To the matter at hand. Let's see what we can find out about Dr. Stonebridge and his friend the philanthropist and the island of Naxos."

Before too long, Mallory had discovered an extravagant photo-spread on the website of a San Francisco tabloid about Dimitri Dimitriou's fund-raising party for Special Education — the one at which Rafael had met Dr.

Stonebridge.

It seemed to have been the social event of the year. Mallory scrolled down and down, amazed at the number of pictures. She then went back to the top. The first photographs were of the estate itself – the main house and guest house, the gardens, the lighthouse rising majestically against a brilliantly blue sky.

To Mallory's surprise and delight, all of the buildings had been whitewashed in the Greek style, and there were stone walkways everywhere that looked as though they belonged on a Greek island. There was a small building with a domed roof, archways leading to interior courtyards, and brightly painted wooden shutters that could be closed to keep out the weather.

"I don't know a lot about modern Greek architecture," Mallory said. "Well, practically nothing. But I've seen pictures of towns on various Greek islands, particularly Mykonos, and Dimitri Dimitriou's estate might have been built there."

"Can you show me some pictures?" Jupiter asked.

Quickly, Mallory pulled up images of white buildings crowded on a hillside, resplendent against a blue sky and a dark ocean.

"I see what you mean," Jupiter said. "But those buildings on Mykonos look so crowded. Even I can see how well-spaced, well-designed, and interesting the buildings on Mr. Dimitriou's estate seem to be."

"There's the lighthouse Dr. Stonebridge told us about," Mallory said, "and the artificial island on which it's built."

"And the arched stone bridge from the mainland," Jupiter said.

Mallory noticed that there was also a big dock near the island where a fair-sized yacht was moored, and some smaller boats – possibly rowboats – upside down on a sandy beach. There was also a shallow cave at the bottom of a cliff. The tabloid had run a caption under the cave that read "A pirate's paradise!"

What a place! Mallory thought. Of course, it couldn't have been built without a great deal of money, but wealth alone would never have led to this result. In Mallory's observation, wealth often led to vulgarity and ostentation. In order to create something like Dimitriou's estate, you had to have passion, education, and, above all, a sense of proportion, history, and taste. And, on top of all that, Dimitriou was a philanthropist!

Below the estate were photos of the people who had attended the gala. Mallory quickly found a picture of Dimitri Dimitriou himself, with his arm around the shoulders of another man identified as Stavros Economides, the estate manager. Dimitriou was very handsome, Mallory thought, with a head of thick dark hair, intense eyes, and noble features.

Economides was somehow blunter, a bit shorter, with a brushy mustache and very bright teeth. He looked very Greek and very hearty, and both men were smiling for the camera, but Mallory instantly knew that, of the two, she preferred Dimitriou. There was something about Economides's face she didn't quite trust. But since she knew this might be irrational, she didn't mention it to Jupiter. She just said she thought Economides looked a little odd.

"I don't see anything odd about him," Jupiter responded. "He must be the man who lost his wife in the boating accident — after which Mr. Dimitriou brought him to the States and offered him a job. Remember what Dr. Stonebridge said about Mr. Dimitriou — about his loyalty and generosity to old childhood acquaintances. Those men have been friends since they were little boys."

"Look," Mallory said, pointing. "There's

Rafael." He was clearly not a celebrity – not one of the people the tabloid was featuring in its spread – but he was visible in a group of people he might have worked or taught with. It was odd to see him in a jacket and tie.

"And there's Dr. Stonebridge," Jupiter said as Mallory scrolled down the photographs again. The professor looked much like he had yesterday, in a conservative blue blazer, dark slacks, and a striped tie. He was deep in conversation with a woman who looked to Mallory as if she, too, were Greek. She was very beautiful – quite tall, with olive skin, a mane of dark curly brown hair, deep-set eyes, and a regal bearing. The two of them were standing with a few other people.

Mallory was surprised to see how close to the woman Dr. Stonebridge was standing. He looked as though he was quite interested in her.

"I wonder who that is standing next to him," she said.

"The caption says her name is Nikoleta Kyriaku. Sounds pretty Greek. Maybe she's a friend of Mr. Dimitriou," said Jupiter.

"She's a lot younger than Dr. Stonebridge," Mallory said.

"By about thirty years, I'd say," Jupiter

remarked. "And they're clearly not related."

"I got the impression yesterday that romance was the last thing on Dr. Stonebridge's mind," Mallory said.

"Yes," Jupiter said. "He told us he'd never been married, and when I asked if he was in a relationship – maybe that was the wrong word – "

"Anyway," Mallory said, "he certainly told you no."

"In fact, he told me 'no, no, no, no, no,' if I'm remembering correctly," Jupiter said.

"The way people do when they're embarrassed," Mallory said. "Protesting too strongly."

"Exactly," Jupiter said.

"I somehow doubt that woman is his girlfriend," Mallory said, "but it looks like he wouldn't mind if she were."

"Let's see if we can find out more about her," Jupiter said.

Mallory put her name into the search bar. It turned out that Nikoleta Kyriaku was on the administrative staff at UC Santa Barbara and was currently working as a part-time secretary in the Classics Department.

"So that's how he knows her," Jupiter said.

"Yes," Mallory said. "But he still looks interested."

"Is Kyriaku a common Greek name?" Jupiter asked.

"I don't know," Mallory said. She entered the name in her search bar.

As Mallory scanned down the list of results, she was surprised to find a link to the site for Aegean Treasures. She clicked on it.

The browser opened a page with a banner photo of the Acropolis and a brief history of the business. It had been founded fifteen years before in Santa Barbara by Mr. Dimitriou, who had wanted to bring a taste of his native country to his new home. He imported Greek cheese, wine, honey, olives, olive oils, other foodstuffs, and novelty items. The business had been a success from the start and had expanded to stores in San Diego, Santa Monica, and Thousand Oaks.

The business had been managed for over ten years by a man named Achilles Kyriaku. There was a picture of him smiling at the camera while seated at a table. He had been born on Naxos, the text read, and was the oldest son of a large Greek family that had been on the island for generations. He had olive skin, dark curly hair, and looked to be in his fifties.

There was no way of knowing if he was related to Nikoleta, Mallory thought, though they looked alike in several ways. She also had no way of knowing how common a Greek name Kyriaku was.

"Dr. Stonebridge told us Mr. Dimitriou had hired a man from Naxos to run his business," Mallory remarked to Jupiter.

"A man who was happy to take the job," Jupiter said, "because of the economic situation in Greece. We should write this down, as Bob suggested. Perhaps Chris Markos can tell us what he knows about the Kyriaku family and if Achilles and Nikoleta are related."

"I guess it's a place to start," Mallory said, "though I'm not sure what, if anything, this might have to do with the rumors about Dr. Stonebridge."

"To investigate those," Jupiter said, "we'd have to question the people who Rafael heard them from. And at the moment, I'd be surprised if the theft of the Minoan treasure didn't take precedence."

Just then, Bob came hurrying over to them, holding a brown paper bag. "It's my lunchtime," Bob said. "Can you guys take a break?"

"Sure," Mallory said. "This is a good

time." She closed her laptop, stuck it in her backpack, and followed Bob and Jupiter outside. The picnic table in front was unoccupied, so the three hurried to it and settled down in the shade of a tree Mallory had recently learned was called a crepe myrtle.

As they each opened the bag they'd brought and started eating, Mallory filled Bob in on what they'd learned about Mr. Dimitriou's estate, the party he'd thrown, and the people who had been there.

Just as Mallory was finishing, Bob's cellphone rang. He looked at it, puzzled, clearly not expecting a call.

"Hello?" he said. "Oh, hi, Rafael."

He listened carefully, then said, "Just a minute. I'm with Jupiter and Mallory at the library. Let me tell them what you said. Then I'll put the phone down so that everyone can listen."

He quickly filled them in. Rafael had just gotten off the phone with Dr. Stonebridge. The professor had returned to Santa Barbara the night before and had awakened to news of the robbery. He'd just been contacted by the police, who wanted to interview him tomorrow, at his house.

"He's a bit jittery," Rafael said, his voice

sounding tinny and far away. Mallory could barely hear him over the noise of traffic. "He's normally very calm, but he's obviously quite shocked. I would be too, if I were in his situation. The police have asked him to go to a local laboratory and give a DNA sample."

Jupiter started. "Why do they want him to do that?"

"Your guess is as good as mine," Rafael said. "They didn't explain their request. But they did say it would take twenty-four hours to sequence the sample and they wanted to compare it to a sample they already have."

"Did they tell him what the other sample was?" Bob asked. "Is it connected to the robbery?"

"They didn't tell him anything," Rafael said. "But *I* told him to call a lawyer right away. He said he thought that would be silly, since he hadn't done anything to be ashamed of."

"Ashamed of?" Jupiter said. "That's hardly the point."

"What he meant," Rafael said, "is that he isn't guilty of anything."

"Nevertheless," Mallory said, "just because he knows he's innocent doesn't mean the police will think he's innocent."

"Exactly," Bob said. "When I first saw his photograph on the Classics Department's website, I thought he looked rather naïve and unworldly."

That was being charitable, Mallory thought. She'd never liked or trusted the police, or anyone who acted in that sort of position of authority. They tended to think they *were* the law rather than representatives of it, and they could get drunk on their own power. Though Mallory couldn't remember any specific incident in her childhood which had made her feel that way, she felt it very strongly.

To think that you had nothing to worry about merely because you were innocent − . Right now she knew that plenty of innocent men and women were sitting in jails and prisons, having their lives wasted, she thought.

"Anyway," Rafael said. "Though he refused to call his lawyer, he actually joked that I could represent him, if necessary − because Elena is a paralegal. But he seemed much more open to involving the four of you when I mentioned you again. He said that maybe it *would* be a good idea for you to poke around a little bit and see what you could uncover. Perhaps you could come up with ideas as to how to help him, if indeed he needs help."

"Yes," Jupiter said. "We'll head up to-morrow – "

"That's just it," Rafael said. "That was the original plan, but everything's changed now because of the robbery and the call from the police. I've managed to get the four of you a suite in one of the dormitories, starting any time you want to check in. I think it would be good for us to get up to Santa Barbara as soon as possible. Could the four of you leave today? I know you were planning to have Worthington take you, but I could take you myself if you can leave this afternoon. That way we could all be there with Dr. Stonebridge in the morning when the police get there to interview him."

Mallory's pulse quickened. The case was picking up speed. "I can go," she said.

"I as well," Jupiter said. "Though we'll all need a bit of time to pack."

"We were supposed to call Chris Markos, our friend on Naxos, in about an hour and a half. Can we leave after that?" Bob asked.

"Sure," Rafael said. "That will work."

"Pete's still at the Rescue Center," Bob said. "He was planning to bike to the Salvage Yard in time for the call, and he won't have his gear for the trip with him."

"I'll pick him up at the Center," Rafael said, "take him home, then bring him to the Salvage Yard for the phone call. In the meantime, the three of you should get there as well. I'll take Bob and Mallory home, so you can pack too. Then the two of you can bike back to the Salvage Yard to talk to Chris. I've got something to do downtown, and then we can all head up to Santa Barbara together."

Wow! Mallory thought. This was happening fast. She'd have to leave a note for her mother, but she was sure that would be all right.

"As a famous detective once remarked," Jupiter said. 'The game's afoot!'"

5

A Virtual Visit To Greece

So much had happened since Rafael had unexpectedly shown up at the Rescue Center that Pete felt almost breathless. After hearing the astounding news about the robbery and the sudden change of plans, Pete had gotten into Rafael's truck and they'd sped across town to his house. His mother was surprised that Pete was leaving a day early, but he explained everything to her while he packed a bag. Then he and Rafael were off to the Salvage Yard, where they arrived only minutes after Mallory, Bob, and Jupiter had gotten there.

When Rafael had told Pete that Dr. Stonebridge was under suspicion for the theft of the Minoan Treasure, Pete had been quite upset. Though he'd only met the man once, he'd really liked him, and he now felt badly about judging him from a photograph and calling him a nerd before they'd even met.

In fact, what with one thing and another, Pete suddenly felt quite sorry for Dr. Stonebridge. He also thought it was pretty ironic that all of this was happening on the day that he, Bob, and Jupiter were going to be talking for the first time, by Skype, to Christos Markos.

When The Three Investigators had been involved in the mystery surrounding Skeleton Island and had first met Chris, he had also been wrongly suspected of something he hadn't done – and just as Pete had been sure that Chris Markos had been innocent, so, too, he was sure that Dr. Stonebridge was.

"I've got to take off now," Rafael said. "But I'll be back by the time your call is done. Mallory, Bob, hop in the truck. I'll grab your wheels. Can you manage your bikes with your backpacks on?"

"You bet," Bob said.

"All right," said Rafael. "Let's go."

After they left, Jupiter took off, too – through the gate at the back of the Salvage Yard – to pack his bags.

Pete just had time to notice that, in the flurry of excitement, Mallory had left her messenger bag on the porch of the Salvage Yard Office when suddenly the bag rang – or rather, the cellphone in its outside pocket did.

Pete stared at it for a minute, wondering whether the call was important. What if it was Mallory's mother? He decided he'd better answer it, just to be safe. He reached over, grabbed Mallory's phone out of its pocket, flipped it open, and said "Hello?"

Pete was taken aback when instead he heard a familiar voice he couldn't quite identify saying, "Who's that? I was calling Mallory MacLeod."

"Mallory's not here right now," Pete said. "This is Pete Crenshaw. Can I take a message?"

At that, he heard a rush of laughter, and then, "Pete! It's Califia!"

Jeez, thought Pete. He should have known at once. Although he and Califia had never been in the same class at school, they had been in the same grade for almost as long as he could remember.

Her mother was a dancer and her father was an actor; Califia wanted to be an actor, too. She was bi-racial, very pretty, and very nice, and the summer before, Pete had gotten to know her better when she played Juliet in a production of *Romeo and Juliet* at the Rocky Beach Theatre Festival. He'd developed a serious crush on her.

But while Pete wasn't normally shy around girls and had had a number of sort-of-girlfriends, since the young Indian actor Daman Duwalia had been playing Romeo to Califia's Juliet, and Pete knew that Califia had been quite smitten, he hadn't made a move of any kind. This was partly because Pete had a sort of man-crush on Daman, too – but mostly because he just couldn't imagine that Daman wouldn't return Califia's feeling, and if he did, then clearly Pete didn't have a chance. But just recently, Mallory had told him that the whole Califia-Daman thing had ended a long time ago.

"Califia!" he said, flushing a little. "How *are* you?"

"Good!" Califia said. "Really good."

For a moment, Pete didn't know what to say. Finally, he managed, "Are you doing another play this summer?"

"I am, actually," Califia said. "A new comedy called 'The Gods.' It's a sort of French farce about the gods of ancient Greece. You know, Apollo and Artemis and Poseidon and Zeus and Aphrodite. I play Aphrodite. I tried out for Demeter or Athena, but I guess I've already been typecast!" She laughed.

Pete had only the vaguest idea of who Demeter and Aphrodite were, but he knew who Athena was. The very first case that Mallory had been involved with had featured a book called *Athena, Goddess of Wisdom.* So he managed to say, "I don't know. I think you'd be great as the Goddess of Wisdom!"

He couldn't believe how embarrassed and awkward he felt. He was relieved when Califia said, in response to his feeble compliment, "That's really nice of you, Pete. I'm just calling because Mallory left a message saying that you guys are heading for Santa Barbara. Have The Three Investigators got a case?"

"Well, maybe. We hope so," Pete said. "It's about Greek stuff, too, actually. The Museum of Classical Antiquities up there was having an exhibit of an amazing bunch of gold jewelry called the Minoan Treasure, and it was stolen last night by two men with masks."

"You're kidding," Califia said – sounding astounded but also quite impressed.

"No," Pete said. "And a friend of Rafael Solares, who we met last summer on the animal smuggling case – a Classics professor named Dr. Stonebridge – has asked us to look into rumors that he may be a treasure smuggler! He isn't, but he does spend half the year in Greece, on archeological digs, and he was part of the team that found the Minoan Treasure in the first place. Right now, we're waiting to make a Skype call to a friend of ours who lives on the island where Dr. Stonebridge got his start."

Now Califia sounded *really* impressed.

"You have a friend who lives on a Greek island?" she asked.

"Well, a sort of friend," Pete said. "We met him on an island off the coast of Florida. It was called Skeleton Island, and at one point Bob and Chris and I were all trapped together in an underwater cavern. We found a bunch of gold doubloons – pirate doubloons – and we lost track of time, and the tide came in and ended up jamming Chris's boat against the mouth of the cavern. That sort of thing can make you into a friend really fast – and then later Chris rescued me and Bob from the bad guys."

"Wow," said Califia. "I'm amazed I've never heard any of this before."

"It was back in the days before Bob was writing up our cases for our website," Pete told her. He was about to explain more when Jupiter arrived back at the office with his luggage.

This time, Pete blushed outright as Jupiter looked questioningly at Mallory's cellphone.

"Anyway," he said to Califia. "It was great to talk with you, and I'll tell Mallory you called, but I've got to go now."

"That's fine," Califia said. "But I want to hear that story about Skeleton Island someday!"

They said goodbye, and Pete clicked Mallory's phone shut, then explained to Jupiter why he had answered it in the first place.

It wasn't long before Mallory and Bob both got back to the Salvage Yard, and when they did, Pete told Mallory about Califia's call. He felt oddly naked when she glanced at him quizzically, and even Bob seemed to be giving him a bit of side-eye. He was glad it was time to make the Skype call.

In Headquarters, Bob pushed the desktop computer out of the way so that he could set his laptop, with its built-in camera, in its place. Pete arranged two chairs on one side of the desk facing the screen, so that Chris could see both of them. He sat down next to Bob, who quickly brought up the Skype interface and signed in. Jupiter and Mallory stood behind them for the time being.

Bob clicked "Calls" and then chose "Greece" from the drop-down menu. He entered the telephone number Chris had given him and then clicked CALL.

Pete was smiling, staring at the blank screen, and then all of a sudden there was

Christos Markos, looking suntanned and happy and a few years older than Pete remembered. He'd let his curly black hair grow longer and he wore a red and white striped tee-shirt.

"Chris!" Bob said. "I'm sorry we're late."

"Do not worry about that," Chris said. "I am so happy to see the two of you!"

Though Chris filled most of the screen, Pete could get glimpses of his room behind him. An old fishing net had been hung on the wall over the single bed, its cork buoys colorfully painted. The walls were white, the color of the whitewash that Pete had seen in pictures of Greek villages. The bedspread was a vibrant blue. This was the first time Pete had ever been involved in a Skype call, and it took a bit of getting used to.

"Who is that behind you?" Chris asked.

"It's Jupiter and a new friend of ours," Pete said. "Say hi, guys."

Pete and Bob shoved their chairs aside so that Jupiter and Mallory could see the screen better.

"Jupiter!" Chris said. "You look different!"

"Hello, Chris," Jupiter said. "I'm taller and thinner but otherwise the same. We wanted you to meet our new friend Mallory

MacLeod. She's now a Special Consultant to The Three Investigators.”

“Wow!” Chris said. “That is very cool. Congratulations, Mallory!”

Mallory said a few quick things and then Jupiter told Pete and Bob to get on with the call. He and Mallory would be right there on the other side of the desk if they were needed.

Pete and Bob resettled their chairs. Chris was so excited to be talking to them that he was almost bouncing up and down.

“What time is it on Naxos?” Pete asked. He glanced at his watch. “Wow! It's almost two here – ”

“We are ten hours later,” Chris said. “It is almost midnight, but do not worry. I will not go to sleep for some time. It's summer, and here everyone stays up late and sleeps until the middle of the morning while it is still cool. My father and I did not even finish dinner until 10:30.”

“It's great to see you, Chris,” Bob said. “How is everything?”

“It is good to be back in Greece,” Chris said. “It is better than Florida at the moment. And the diving business is doing pretty well – many tourists who want to learn. Since the accident, my father still cannot dive, but I am happy to help and he hires other people too, so we do his diving for him. Sometimes we have trouble paying for the shop we rent on the oceanfront where we run the business. But on the whole I cannot complain."

"I'm glad to hear things are going well," Bob said. "It's an amazing coincidence, but we got your e-mail just before we were introduced to a man named Dr. Stonebridge. He's an archaeologist who started his career years ago, on Naxos of all places. So we're also calling because we may need your help getting him out of a jam he may be getting into."

"Sure!" Chris said cheerfully. "Anything for The Three Investigators."

Pete and Bob took turns filling Chris in on what was going on. When they got to the theft of the Minoan Treasure, Chris looked shocked.

"I had not heard of this," he said.

"And the police think maybe Dr. Stonebridge is involved," Pete said. "They asked him to give a DNA sample and tomorrow morning the police are meeting with him. We're going to be there."

"I do not see how I can help you," Chris said. "After all, you are there and I am here."

All of a sudden, Pete was not sure how

Chris could help them, either.

Then Jupiter spoke up.

"Bob, remember all the stuff that Mallory and I told you at lunch. Chris could help with that."

"Yes," Bob said, leaning forward earnestly. "We don't know exactly what kind of help we need, but you're there, as you said, on Naxos, where this story really started."

"Every time Dr. Stonebridge is back in Greece, he visits Naxos, where he has lots of friends," Mallory said. "Maybe Chris could find out who those people are."

"Did you hear that, Chris?" Pete asked.

"Yes," Chris said. He wrote something down on a pad of paper.

"And maybe he could do some research on Dimitri Dimitriou and the Kyriaku family," Jupiter added. "Anything at all he found out would be useful."

"Who?" Chris asked. "I cannot hear very well."

Jupiter got up and hurried around to face the screen.

"The Greek businessman from Naxos who helped bring the treasure to the United States," he said. "Dimitri Dimitriou."

"I have heard of him," Chris said.

"Everyone on Naxos has."

"Also the Kyriaku family," Jupiter said.

Chris quickly wrote the names down on his pad.

"I do not know much about them," Chris said, "though I have heard the name. I think it is a big family, and some members of it run a construction business on the island. I have seen trucks with that name on them. But I am happy to ask people and to look around."

"That would be great," Pete said as Jupiter returned to his seat.

"What have you heard about Mr. Dimitriou?" Bob asked.

"He was born on Naxos," Chris said. "Before he moved to America many years ago, he was already a very successful businessman. He made a huge pile of drachmas building yachts that powerful Russians and American millionaires bought. Now he buys things from Naxos and other places in Greece and sells them in America – food and wine and oil."

"That's what we heard, too," Bob said. "Jupiter and Mallory discovered that Mr. Dimitriou has brought this Achilles Kyriaku to work for him in California. He's also brought childhood friends of his who needed help."

"Yes," Chris said. "Everyone says how

good he is to Naxos. He gives money to schools here, and he set up a health clinic and helped local businesses. He is famous for helping his friends. And he loves everything Greek, especially Greek history and culture. He is very proud of where he was born. He comes back to Naxos every year for a month or more."

"Ask him if Mr. Dimitriou has a place of his own on Naxos," Mallory asked.

"Is that Mallory?" Chris said, smiling. "I heard that! I do not know for sure, but I do not think so. I have heard that he stays with friends when he is here. If he does own a house, it is a small one. He used to own quite a big house on the ocean, with its own private lighthouse, but he sold that when he moved to America."

Wow! Pete thought. Another lighthouse. Or rather, a first one!

"Everyone in Greece loves lighthouses," Chris said. "Of course they are very important as we are a seagoing people and the islands are many and rocky. The sailor must be careful. My father told me that our ancestors believed that the four elements of the world came together in a lighthouse. Earth for the stony ground that they are built on and the rock they are built of, water for the sea they stand next to, air for the air they reach into, and fire for the fire that burns at the top."

Pete remembered that Rafael had mentioned earth, air, fire, and water the other day, and how much Rafael had liked the idea that all things were made of just those four classical elements.

"I do not even know if Mr. Dimitriou's lighthouse is still standing," Chris went on. "His house was on the other side of the island, quite far from Naxos Town where we live. This is a big island – the largest in the Cyclades."

That surprised Pete a little; he usually thought of islands as being small. But then he remembered that Australia – a whole continent – was also an island.

"There is a famous story on Naxos," Chris said. "My father told it to me when I was a boy, and all my friends heard it too. They even tell the story in school now, because it is about friendship and generosity. When Mr. Dimitriou was eleven years old, he and a friend were diving for oysters quite far from Naxos Town. They would sell them to restaurants if they were lucky and found them.

"They were both wearing sandals because the sea floor is sometimes very rocky, and Mr. Dimitriou's sandal got caught between two rocks and he could not get loose," Chris continued. "Because of the currents, he also could not swim down and take off the sandal, so he was very scared and in a lot of trouble. The more he struggled, the more the sandal got wedged."

"Yikes!" Pete said. "At least I'm glad to know he got out O.K."

"Yes," Chris said. "His friend swam down again and again and couldn't get the sandal off either. The water was very rough. Finally he took his oyster knife and cut the sandal straps loose so that Mr. Dimitriou could shoot to the surface. It was a very close call for both of them. They almost drowned. The friend surely saved Mr. Dimitriou's life. That is why it is such a famous story – about thinking of others before you think of yourself."

"That's a great story," Pete said. He hoped *he* would do anything he could to help his friends if they were in danger, even if he was scared and in danger himself.

"I do not know who the friend was, but I have heard that when they were much older and the friend was in trouble, Mr. Dimitriou did whatever he could to help him."

"Was the boy's name Achilles Kyriaku?" Bob asked.

"I do not know," Chris said, "but if you

can hold on for a moment, I will do some research on some websites that use only the Greek language and then call you back."

The screen went dark and then returned to the Skype interface.

"Boy," Pete said. "He's certainly on the case."

Bob looked a little taken aback by the abrupt end of the call.

"I hope he doesn't take very long," Jupiter said. "We don't have all day. Rafael will be here soon."

Pete's stomach clenched and he gripped his legs with his hands. But all of a sudden, there was Chris's face again.

"Yes," he said. "You were right, Bob. The man who saved Mr. Dimitriou is Achilles Kyriaku! It says he manages Mr. Dimitriou's business, called Aegean Treasures, that the big main store is in Santa Barbara, and that he lives there."

"That's great work, Chris," Bob said. "Thanks!"

"And fast!" Pete said. He glanced at his watch. As much as he didn't want to end the call, he realized that Jupiter had been right and that Rafael would be getting back at any moment. He mentioned this to Bob.

"Chris," Bob said. "We've got to go, I'm sorry to say."

"We're heading up to Santa Barbara this afternoon," Pete said, "to see if we can help Dr. Stonebridge."

"We can talk again soon," Chris said, "now that we know how to do it! I will do the work you ask − and I will certainly find out as much as I can about the Kyriakus."

"Thanks, Chris," Pete said. "Boy, it's good to see you! Talk to you soon."

As they cut the call, Jupiter jumped to his feet. All four of them were pumped up about the call − Jupiter perhaps most of all.

"Bob," he said. "Would you look up the address of Aegean Treasures in Santa Barbara? Maybe it will be on our way."

"Sure, Jupe," Bob said. He jotted down the address and slipped it into his portfolio.

Just as they hurried out of Headquarters, Rafael was pulling into the Salvage Yard. Mallory and Bob climbed in front with Rafael, and Jupiter and Pete crawled into the back under the truck cap. It was comfortable back there, with a futon on the floor and lots of pillows. All their gear was back there, too, so it was a little crowded. But Pete didn't mind − although oddly enough, after he had settled himself in comfort on the futon, instead of thinking about having seen Chris again after all this time, he found himself thinking about Califia, and how impressed she had seemed with his story about Skeleton Island.

Pete would actually have enjoyed thinking about Califia for the whole trip up to Santa Barbara, but once they were on the road, Jupiter opened the sliding window between the front seat and the truck cap and asked Rafael if he would be willing to enter the address of Aegean Treasures into his smart phone.

It turned out that – as Jupe had hoped – the store was on their way to the UC Santa Barbara campus, and they made plans to stop and check it out.

Wrenching his mind away from Califia and back to the case, Pete asked Jupiter why he wanted to stop at the store, anyway.

"Do you want to meet Mr. Kyriaku?" he asked.

"There's no reason to think he'll be there," Jupiter said. "But it's always a good idea to assemble as many facts as you can when you're beginning a case."

Pete thought that was probably true. He lay back on the pillows and closed his eyes. It had been a hectic and exciting day, and he was feeling a little tired. He thought he'd just take a rest. He woke up with a start when the truck came to a stop. He sat up, rubbing his eyes. "Where are we?" he asked.

"We're in Santa Barbara," Jupiter said. "Let's go."

Rafael stayed in his truck as Pete and the others got out. Pete discovered that they were on East Montecito Street. Across from where Rafael had parked was a storefront with the words Aegean Treasures in gilt-edged black letters on the plate glass window over which hung an awning with blue and white stripes. As they opened the shop's door, a bell jangled.

"Wow!" Pete said. "What a place!"

The store was spacious and brightly lit, with polished wooden floors and pin spots high overhead accenting large wooden barrels of Greek olives and arrangements of shiny tins of Greek olive oil. Behind the front counter stood a young man who might have been Chris Markos's older brother.

"Hallo," he called as they walked in. "Are you looking for something in particular?" he asked.

"No, thank you," Jupiter said. "Just browsing."

Looking around, Pete saw cases of

Greek cheeses, shelves of honey from different parts of the country, shelves of wine, tinned fish and eggplant and octopus and other Greek specialties Pete had never heard of. In the back of the store were all sorts of non-food items with cards in nearby metal stands describing what they were.

Pete suddenly saw something that looked familiar. "Hey, guys," he said. "Come look at this!" It was a display of silver bracelets, one exactly like the next. Pete picked one up and examined it closely. "Doesn't this look to you like the one Dr. Stonebridge was wearing?"

Jupiter came over and held one in his palm. "Very observant, Second," he said. "Good for you. This is exactly the bracelet Dr. Stonebridge was wearing. He must have gotten it here."

Pete was happy to have seen the bracelet first, and he kept reading the sign connected to the display. "It says you can have your initials stamped on the bracelet, right here in the store," he said. "In Greek or English. Though I bet most people choose Greek."

"That's part of the mystery solved," Jupiter said, "but it doesn't explain why a man like Dr. Stonebridge would be wearing such a thing. This is a great find. Let's fan out and see if we can discover anything else of interest."

Pete started walking around the store looking at the various things Aegean Treasures had for sale. There were ocean-polished rocks from the Mediterranean, belly dancing hip scarves, Greek fishermen's caps, small dolls dressed in traditional Greek costumes, wooden blocks for children with a different Greek letter on each of their six sides, soap made from olive oil. A lot of the displays had informative cards as well, explaining the history of the item and where it was made.

Pete was looking at the wooden blocks, wondering if there were Greek letters for his initials, when he noticed that Mallory was calling to Jupiter. She was across the store, standing in front of a short wooden barrel on a tabletop. He was about to head over to join them when he got the feeling that Mallory actually wanted to talk to Jupiter in private, so he stayed where he was, though he watched them with interest.

Mallory kept turning back and gesturing at the wooden barrel. At one point she reached in and grabbed a handful of something. She and Jupiter talked animatedly for some time until Pete could hardly stand it.

Then all at once the two of them were

headed up to the main desk and the cash register. What were they buying? Something that had been in the barrel? He called to Bob and the two of them went to join Jupiter and Mallory. By the time Pete got to the register, they had bought whatever they were buying and were ready to leave.

"Let's go," Jupiter said brightly, though his voice sounded a little false to Pete. Mallory was holding a small brown paper bag, crimped at the top. As they waked out of Aegean Treasures onto the sidewalk, Pete could see that Rafael was still in the truck, waiting for them.

"What did you buy?" Pete asked. "What's in the bag?"

Jupiter looked at him a little sternly. "Just wait a minute or two," he said, "until we're back in the truck."

"Why?" Pete asked, flustered. "What's up? Is it a secret?"

Jupiter lowered his voice. "Just keep walking and act natural. I don't want anyone in the store to notice anything particular about the way we're acting."

Of all the things Jupiter might have said, that was the last thing Pete expected. He was thunderstruck. Whoa! he thought. What *was* in that brown paper bag?

6

Mallory Makes An Amazing Discovery

Bob had also observed the secretive goings-on between his friends. He'd been looking at a display of evil-eye jewelry when Mallory called Jupiter over to join her. Interested by what he was reading on the information card, he stayed where he was − though he frequently glanced up at what looked to be a lively conversation.

Since normally Pete would have been interested in joining them, Bob wondered if he might have something on his mind at the moment other than the case.

He'd certainly looked a little peculiar when Bob and Mallory had gotten back to the Salvage Yard. Pete had told Mallory that Califia García-Williams had called her on her cellphone, and that Pete had picked up and talked with her. Since he and Pete had ended up in two different parts of Rafael's pickup truck for the drive up to Santa Barbara, Bob had had no chance to grill him about what had actually happened.

And now, something else was clearly going on − something very immediate, which

112

seemed to be occupying both Jupiter and Mallory. As they hurried across the street toward Rafael's pickup truck, Jupiter looked relieved.

"Sorry I barked at you back there," he said to Pete. "I just wanted us all to remain calm and composed. You'll understand soon."

"I hope so!" said Pete. "What's going on?"

"We'll tell you once we hit the road," Mallory said. They all climbed back into Rafael's pick-up.

"Did you find out anything interesting?" Rafael asked curiously as Bob sat next to him and Mallory sat by the window.

"I don't think we found *out* anything," Bob said, "but it seems as though Mallory and Jupiter found *something* that was interesting. Come on, Mallory. What's in the bag?"

"You're not going to believe it," she said. "It's so amazing."

She seemed to be trying to figure out how best to explain her thoughts as Rafael pulled into traffic and drove through Santa Barbara on his way back to the highway.

Bob was surprised at how many towering palm trees dotted the sides of the streets. To the east, the mountains rose, their flanks dappled with shadows. Just then, Bob sensed something moving in his peripheral vision. He turned and saw Pete's face in the window between the truck cab and the back. He looked as if he was going to pop.

"I think you should open the window," Mallory said to Bob. "There's no reason to torture poor Pete any longer."

Bob tugged on the latch, and the window slid back.

"Thanks!" Pete said. "O.K., Mallory. Out with it. Jupiter's not saying a thing. He told me it was your find. What does that mean?"

"Well," said Mallory. "Do you remember what Dr. Stonebridge told us about tetradrachms? Those ancient silver coins with the head of Alexander the Great on them? They sell reproductions of them in Aegean Treasures. That's what was in that barrel I was looking through — a whole barrel of reproduction coins. I was reading the card by the barrel explaining what the coins were, and then I started absent-mindedly fishing through the coins. I was interested to see that the reproductions weren't identical. I mean, they were more or *less* identical, but if you looked carefully, there were subtle differences one from the other."

"Why would they do that?" Pete asked

from behind Bob's head. "It doesn't really make sense. If there was a bucket full of quarters, they'd all look exactly alike."

"Not really," Mallory said. "Depending on how long the quarters had been in circulation, some would be worn down more than others. And depending on the mint where they were made, there might have been other variations. I learned from the card that there were different mints in ancient Greece as well."

"So some of the coins in the barrel were worn down?" Pete asked.

"Better than that," Mallory said. "It turned out that there were four basic models. My guess is that they did that so that people wouldn't buy just one. When they saw that there were four kinds, they wouldn't be able to make up their minds and might buy all four. And if there were four of them, then they wouldn't so obviously be reproductions."

"How much were they?" Bob asked.

"Fifteen dollars apiece," Mallory said.

"Fifteen dollars!" Pete said. "For a worthless piece of money?"

"It does seem like a lot," Mallory said. "But these are really high quality, like something you might buy in a museum gift shop."

"So you bought four?" Bob asked.

"Where'd you get the money?"

"Jupiter said he always keeps a hundred dollars of Three Investigators money in his wallet for times just like these," Mallory said. "We bought five."

"Five?" Bob said.

Mallory uncrimped the bag on her lap, reached in, fished around, and pulled out four coins. Bob found himself holding two of them as Mallory handed the other two to Pete.

"Wow!" Pete said. "These are great!"

Bob examined the coins carefully. They were thick and heavy in the hand, silvery in color – though Bob was sure they weren't actually made of silver. One side showed the head of Alexander the Great in bas-relief, as though his head had arisen from the metal background. Alexander had a large nose and full cheeks and he was wearing a military helmet from which flames or feathers seemed to be shooting. His likeness extended to the very edges of the coin.

Bob flipped the coin over. "What's this on the back?" he asked.

"It's hard to see, isn't it?" Mallory said. "The card I read said it was a likeness of Zeus. He's seated in a chair with a jug at his feet and his hand outstretched holding what looks to be an owl."

Bob looked at the second coin Mallory had given him. It was substantially the same, though the head of Alexander seemed different, somehow. The impression it gave was less of nobility than of youth. The differences were subtle.

"This is a weird thing to say," Pete said, "but they remind me a little of those paving stones that are all a little bit different from one another."

Instantly Bob knew exactly what Pete meant. "Yes!" Bob said. "Each one has a pattern that's like the others, but when you put them down, there's enough variation so that it looks like real quarried stone and not like something manufactured in a factory."

"That's a great comparison," Mallory said. "In a barrel full of real Alexander tetradrachms, each one would be different. After all, they'd have been around, in someone's pocket or box or in the ground, for well over two thousand years, getting abraded and damaged."

"Why did you call them Alexander tetradrachms?" Bob asked. "Is there another kind?"

"Yes, as a matter of fact," Mallory said.

"The card I read said that the older tetradrachms, minted before Alexander, obviously didn't have his head on them. They had Athena on one side and the Owl of Athena on the other."

"The Owl of Athena!" Pete said.

"That's on Li Chang's gravestone!" Bob said. "And on the cover of *Athena, Goddess of Wisdom*. The book he learned Greek from."

"That's really weird!" said Pete. "I was just telling Califia about that book. She told me the play she's in this summer is some sort of comedy about the Greek gods. She tried out for Athena, but she got the role of Aphrodite instead. I'd never heard of Aphrodite, so I tried to keep myself from looking like an idiot by saying she would have been great as the Goddess as Wisdom!"

O.K. Bob thought. He'd been right in thinking there was something a little peculiar about the way Pete had talked about his conversation with Califia. A bit of light grilling would be in order later on.

But Mallory had been listening to Pete attentively, too, and now she put a halt to her own story to ask, "You've really never heard of Aphrodite? Did Califia say anything about her?"

"All she said was that she was afraid she was getting typecast," Pete said. "But I didn't know what she meant, and I didn't want to ask."

At this, both Bob and Mallory burst out laughing, and even Rafael chuckled a bit.

"Aphrodite was the goddess of love and sex and beauty," Mallory explained. "I'm surprised that Califia said that. To say you're getting typecast as *that* seems a bit obnoxious."

Since Pete looked surprised at this observation, Bob jumped in. "I think all she meant was that Juliet was all about love and beauty, and she didn't want to get stuck playing roles that were the same. I think all actors want to stretch themselves when they act," he said.

Given what a bad actor *he* was, Bob could only hope this was true – and he was glad when Jupiter, who had been silent through the whole discussion, suddenly spoke from the back of the truck.

"We seem to have gotten off track here," he said. "The point at the moment isn't Califia, but Mallory. And Pete and Bob seem to be surprisingly slow on the uptake at the moment. I'd have thought you would have remembered the way Mallory noticed in the first case of last summer that the two Chinese talismans we had thought were identical were actually somewhat different. In the second case, she saw that what we thought was a reproduction of a famous 19th century quilt wasn't a reproduction at all, but the original," he added.

It suddenly began to dawn on Bob what was going on here.

With a rising sense of excitement, he said, "Holy smoke. Is the fifth coin you bought an actual Alexander tetradrachm?"

"Unless I've lost my powers," Mallory said, smiling. "I was digging through the barrel and I'd decided there were really only four kinds when my hand felt one that seemed different. I pulled it out and looked at it. What I was holding wasn't a reproduction. It was a real honest-to-goodness Alexander tetradrachm, minted in Greece over two thousand years ago."

She collected the four reproductions and put them back in the bag. Then she pulled out the fifth coin and handed it to Bob.

Bob knew that he'd never have known with Mallory's certainty that this was a real coin, and yet, now that he had it pointed out to him, he could see all the ways it seemed entirely different from the others. When Pete asked, he handed it to him, too, and when, after oohing and ahhing about it, Pete handed it back, he asked Rafael when they would be getting to the dorm.

"It won't be long now," Rafael said. "The campus is about ten miles north of the city. Take a look out the side window and keep your eyes open. It's beautiful – lots of views of the ocean. I think you'll like it. But maybe before we get there, we should stop for a late lunch."

This suggestion made Pete very happy, and soon they were all sitting inside a roadside cafe, eating and talking. Mallory had brought the bag containing the five coins into the cafe with her, and although Rafael had been relatively silent on the drive, once they were all sitting together, eating, he suddenly started talking.

"That's quite a find, Mallory," Rafael said. "How do you think such a thing happened?"

"An accident seems unlikely," she answered. "Though I guess it's possible that the real coin was a model they were using back wherever they were making the reproductions, and it somehow fell into the barrel with the others by mistake."

"Was it the only real coin in the barrel?"

Bob asked.

"I'm not sure," Mallory said. "I didn't look at every one. But its presence made me and Jupiter wonder. Maybe at one time there were a good number of real coins in there, mixed in with the fake ones."

"Very shrewd," Rafael said. "So you think you've uncovered a smuggling operation."

"That's the only thing that makes sense to me and Mallory," Jupiter said. "Our guess is that someone is smuggling real tetradrachms out of Greece in these barrels and is using the reproduction coins as camouflage."

"And when they were going through the barrel and taking out the real coins, they missed one," Bob said.

"Exactly," Mallory said. "If they hadn't missed one, we'd never have stumbled on their scheme."

"How much is the real coin worth?" Bob asked.

"I don't know," Mallory said. "From the research we did and from what Dr. Stonebridge told us, we *do* know that there are a lot of legal Alexander tetradrachms in the world in legal collections and a whole lot still in Greece, waiting to be discovered. They can't be worth a fortune."

"So what's your guess?" Pete said. "You're good at this, especially after all the practice you've had valuing things for the Salvage Yard."

"Maybe two or three hundred dollars a coin," Mallory said.

That wasn't pocket change, Bob thought.

"And if you could gather together, let's say, a thousand of those coins," Jupiter said, "that would be $300,000."

Three hundred thousand dollars! Bob thought. For a thousand small coins that could easily be hidden in a barrel with a mass of other coins that looked almost like them? That was a pretty large profit.

And customs officials – presumably most of whom had never even heard of Alexander tetradrachms – would pose no problem. They would have had little or no experience or training in distinguishing between the real and fake when it came to Greek antiquities. Dr. Stonebridge had been right when he said that the laws on finding Greek treasure were enough to turn the entire population into criminals!

"What do we do now?" Bob asked.

"The four of us have to discuss it," Jupiter said, "but clearly we've stumbled onto something. Between the discovery of the real tetradrachm and the theft of the Minoan treasure, there may be a sophisticated and probably thriving smuggling operation going on up here."

"I never got a chance to see any of the coins," Rafael said now. "Do you think we could put them on the table and study them a bit?"

Bob watched as Mallory carefully spilled the contents of the bag onto the table, then picked up the real Alexander tetradrachm. Rafael offered his hand, palm up, and Mallory placed the coin right in the middle of it.

Rafael looked at it carefully, first one side and then the other. He brought it close to his eye. He rubbed it between his fingers.

"It's an amazing coin," he said. "And even though you were the first – and only! – investigators I thought of when I heard the rumors about Dr. Stonebridge, I'm still impressed by what you've already discovered and deduced."

He handed the genuine coin back to Mallory, then reached out and moved the four reproductions around until all the renditions of Alexander were parallel and facing him. When looked at next to one another like that, Bob could see that the subtle differences among the four separate models were more apparent.

"Look at that!" Rafael said. "Four different Alexanders. One for each of the four investigators. But which of them is which?"

"I'd have to see Pete in a Greek military helmet," Mallory said. "But maybe this one would work for him." She reached out a finger and pulled the third coin out of line. "What do you guys think?"

Bob looked closely at the coin and then compared it with the other three. He thought Mallory might be right. This Alexander looked more unguarded than the others, more enthusiastic − more psyched. It was something about the way the lips were shaped. They seemed to be smiling, while the other three were more sober.

"That's great, Mallory," he said. "Pete as Alexander the Ready-for-Anything."

"I hope that's a compliment!" Pete said.

"You bet it is," Bob said. "Though we can change it to Alexander the Courageous."

Jupiter looked a little uncomfortable − as if he was ready to pay and leave − but when Rafael said, "And which is Mallory's?" he settled back into his seat.

"Let's see," Bob said. He thought about what it was that made Mallory Mallory. Well, there were a lot of things, really. The way she truly saw whatever it was she was looking at. The way she never gave up when she started something. The way she came up with solutions to difficult problems. He picked up the first Alexander Mallory had put down.

When Bob looked at it closely, it seemed that this one was squinting just a little, as though he were seeing further, both into the distance and into the future. He looked calm but assertive and very sure of himself. Bob put it back on the table.

"I'd vote for that one as Mallory's," he said. "Something about the eyes. Alexander the Skeptical."

Now Jupiter looked at it closely. "That's a good call, Bob."

Mallory looked doubtful. "Really?" she asked.

"I agree with Bob and Jupiter," Pete said, picking up one of the two remaining coins. "And this one's Jupiter. Look at that forehead. Exceptionally big brain."

Bob laughed. He had noticed that the brow of the Alexander Pete was referring to looked unusually noble and commanding. Of the four, it was the one that seemed to capture the vision of Alexander and the abilities that had made him such a great leader.

"Pete's right!" he said. "Alexander the Brilliant!"

"Well," Pete said. "I guess there's not much of a question then about which one is yours, Bob."

"That's not true, Pete," Mallory said, picking up the fourth coin and looking at it. "If you hadn't said what you said about the forehead, I was going to nominate this one as Bob's, anyway. This looks like an Alexander who cares about his troops. Who wants them to be properly provisioned and who wants their deeds properly recognized when the battle is over. We could call him Alexander the Careful."

Bob smiled. "Thanks, Mallory. I'll take that."

Just then, the waitress came over with their bill, and after Jupiter had paid it with Three Investigators cash, the five of them got back on the road. They had left Highway One a few minutes ago, after traversing a difficult series of on-ramps and off-ramps that Rafael clearly knew well, and passed Goleta Beach Park. Ahead was a concrete arch that spanned two divided lanes of traffic.

"Here's the Henley Gate," Rafael said. "It's the official entrance to the campus."

Off to the left, Bob could see the Pacific. "Is the campus right on the ocean?" he asked.

"Some of it, yes," Rafael said. "And there are the mountains to the east. As far as location goes, the campus is hard to beat. The rooms I've booked you into are in the new Senior Residence Hall. I think you'll like it. You've got the ocean on one side of you and the campus lagoon on the other."

"There's a lagoon?" Mallory said.

"Yes," Rafael said. "Part saltwater and part fresh water. The crew team uses it. So does the marine science institute."

When the road veered to the right, toward the main campus buildings that Bob could see rising in the distance, Rafael stayed more or less straight, on a small road called Lagoon Road that paralleled the coast.

Bob could see that Pete was looking out the window and pointing out something to Jupiter. He looked pretty charged up.

The residence hall they would be staying in had only three stories, looking more like an apartment building than a dormitory, Bob thought. It was quite attractive, made of brick, with windows that had white stone around them.

"Wow!" said Pete. "This is a lot fancier than I expected!"

"It was built for seniors who want to room together," Rafael said, "but in the summer it's available for anyone who wants to use it. Grab your gear. I'll check you in."

They unloaded their bags from the back of the truck, then walked in the entrance and across a lobby whose bulletin boards were crowded with posters and flyers, to a front desk, behind which a young man sat. He was probably a UCSB student, Bob thought, doing this for a summer job while he also took summer classes.

"Hello," he said in a friendly tone. "Can I help you?"

Rafael showed him some identification and explained that he had booked a suite with three rooms on the second floor, ocean side, for four high school students from the L.A. area.

"Are you here to look at the campus?" the boy asked. "It's a great school."

"We're a little too young for that!" Pete exclaimed. "We've got three more years of high school."

"Well, it's never too early to start thinking about college," the boy said. "If I can help you, let me know."

Bob and the others signed in, and he gave each of them a small packet of information and a room key. "You can get to the suite by the elevator, but you can also take this flight of stairs," he said, gesturing. "Enjoy your stay."

As the five of them moved away from the desk, Rafael said, "Elena and I would like you to come to our house tonight for a bite to eat and a bonfire." He smiled.

"Thanks, Rafael," Mallory said. "That's really nice of you."

"Not really," Rafael said. "Elena is eager to see you again. Why don't you unpack and settle in? I'll be back in an hour or so. I think you'll be surprised at how nice the accommodations are. I'll let you explore them on your own."

Bob hoisted his backpack on his shoulder and grabbed his small bag. Pete, Jupiter, and Mallory did the same, then walked up the stairs – where Bob found that he *was* surprised.

Although they all had keys, there was only a single door, and when Jupiter unlocked it and went in, Bob saw a small living room –

with a couch, two chairs and a table for four –
a tiny kitchen, a bathroom with both a shower
and a tub, and three bedrooms opening onto
the central living area.

One of the bedrooms had two extra-long
twin beds in it, as well as two desks and two
bureaus, and the other two rooms each had a
single bed, desk, and bureau. The beds had
sheets and blankets and pillows, and through a
clever design which involved the hallway to the
bathroom, each of the three bedrooms had
windows facing the ocean, as did the living
room.

It was really a very nice place, and from
Pete's exclamations, he obviously thought so,
too.

"Who's going to get the double?" he
asked. "Why don't Jupe and I take it, so you
two can take the singles? I like rooming with
Jupe. He sleeps so soundly I can always sneak
up on him in the morning!"

"I certainly slept this morning," Jupiter
said. "I dreamed I was in the Olympic games
in ancient Greece." He picked up his bag and
followed Pete into the double, and after Bob
had asked Mallory which of the singles she'd
prefer, Bob went into the other one, dropped
his bag and backpack, and went to stand at the

window. It spanned the entire width of the room. The sun had begun its descent toward the ocean, and the surface of the water was dotted with gold. Bob saw that, when the sun set, it probably flooded the room with light.

But although there was every reason to feel satisfied with both the place they were staying and the way this case was starting out, Bob felt a little blue – maybe because the last time the four of them had been to Santa Barbara together, he'd still held out hope that Mallory would become his girlfriend, and now he knew she never would.

That in itself wouldn't have made him sad – and anyway, *sad* wasn't really the right word for what he felt – but there'd been something about seeing how excited Pete was to have talked to Califia García-Williams. It had made Bob realize that while he and Pete might not have a lot in common when it came to the way they felt about girls, he was just as ready as Pete to meet someone he could get together with.

In that, they were different from Jupiter – who, from the looks of things, was clearly prepared to wait forever for the right girl to come along. It was funny, really, but even after Jupiter had seen how happy Wally and Isabella were to live together in Isabella's house, and how Connor O'Malley and Charlotte Mitchell had hit it off so well after Pete had thought they might, Jupiter seemed impervious to the entire concept.

When Bob and Mallory had been teasing Pete about the fact that he didn't know that Aphrodite was the goddess of love and sex and beauty, Jupiter had said that they seemed to have gotten off track – that the point at the moment wasn't Califia, but Mallory, and that Pete and Bob seemed to be surprisingly slow on the uptake. Hhmm, Bob thought suddenly. Was it possible that Jupiter had been annoyed partly because, at that moment, he'd been feeling *proud* of what Mallory had just done?

7

A Very Innocent Man

It was four hours later, and Jupiter was sitting in Rafael and Elena's backyard, watching the fire in the firepit as the sun set over the ocean in Isla Vista and darkness had started to fall. For a while now, Mallory, Pete, and Bob had been talking about how Pete and Bob had gotten kidnapped the summer before, and the chase in Rafael's boat across the Pacific to Santa Catalina Island. Although Jupiter, too, had vivid memories of that case, for at least ten or fifteen minutes he had been zoning out the chatter and trying to think about the present case, instead.

Although he didn't have much to go on concerning the rumors about Dr. Stonebridge, he was feeling increasingly worried about the danger the professor might be in as a result of his approaching interview with the police. He'd been thinking about the coin Mallory had found at Aegean Treasures. If she was right about both its authenticity and its value − and Jupiter was totally sure she was − then he and she were obviously also right in believing that someone connected to Aegean Treasures was using the business as a front for smuggling.

As the others laughed and bantered, Jupiter wondered fleetingly if the owner of Aegean Treasures – Dr. Stonebridge's friend, Dimitri Dimitriou – could be behind it all, but he quickly discarded that supposition. Not only did Rafael like and trust Dimitriou, but Christos Markos had confirmed his excellent reputation on his home island of Naxos. Besides, Dimitriou was already exceedingly wealthy, and even if thousands of real coins could be imported through Aegean Treasures, there was no way that the profit he would realize from them would add more than a small amount to what he already had.

Could Dimitriou's childhood friend who was now the manager of Aegean Treasures be the culprit? It had to be considered – though it seemed unlikely on the face of it. Why would a man who had been given a new lease on life turn on his old friend and employer?

On the other hand, while the manager of a store – even a chain of four stores – would likely make a good salary, it wouldn't be enough to make him think of himself as rich. Besides, before he had been helped by Dimitriou, he had been the victim of the Greek economy, and he had family back on Naxos who probably needed money. He might have been tempted to add to his salary by bringing in some illegal imports along with the legal ones.

Still, why would he, really? Jupiter wondered. It was more probable that the smuggler was not Achilles Kyriaku but someone who worked for him and was taking advantage of the situation. Or, realistically speaking, a group of people – someone back in Greece to pack the illegal objects with the legal ones, someone in the warehouse in America who could take them out unnoticed, and someone who could distribute the goods in California – a fence.

Jupiter wished he could meet Mr. Dimitriou and Mr. Kyriaku and judge for himself. But for the moment, he thought he ought to look elsewhere for suspects. Besides, the far more pressing issue was the theft of the Minoan Treasure.

Just as he thought this, Elena, who was a paralegal, made a joke about Attorney Rafael Solares and how he would have to protect his client's rights when the police questioned him.

"But *I'm* not a lawyer," Rafael exclaimed, laughing.

"You need to pretend you are," Elena

said, with surprising seriousness. "Keep reminding Dr. Stonebridge that innocent people *do* go to jail. Keep reminding him that he shouldn't say anything. And if the police want to take him downtown, make sure he calls a real lawyer."

"I totally agree with that," Mallory said.

Jupiter did, too. In fact, although there was an antic tone to the discussion, behind it was the sober understanding that Dr. Stonebridge might indeed be in serious trouble – even if he imagined he couldn't possibly be. It would be up to those present (except for Elena, who might actually have been able to help, but who was working the following morning) to save Dr. Stonebridge from whatever might lie in wait.

Not much later, Jupiter suggested they go back to the residence hall. After Rafael had dropped them off and the four of them were back in their suite, Jupiter told the others that before Rafael picked them up and took them to Dr. Stonebridge's house in the morning, he wanted to visit the Classics Department to see what they could find out there. In very short order, they were all in their beds and heading off to sleep.

The next morning, Jupiter slept late.

When he woke and stumbled into the living room, he discovered that Pete had been up practically since dawn and had gone for a walk – first down to the ocean where he'd fished around in tidal pools and then onto the main campus.

"It's so cool, guys," Pete said as he arrived back and the four of them got ready to go find some breakfast. "The University Center is right on the lagoon, and there's a tall tower that has a real carillon, with sixty-one bells!"

Jupiter and the others were fairly quiet as they ate their breakfast in a student cafeteria, but Pete, as usual, was irrepressible. As he talked about the tiny crabs he'd found in one of the tidal pools, Jupiter finally cleared his throat.

"I think we should head over to the Classics Department while we still have time, he said.

"Jeez, Jupe," Pete said. "That won't be as much fun as tiny crabs."

It was a bit of a trek from the residence hall to the building where the Classics Department was housed. There were few people on campus, Jupiter noticed – certainly as compared to the crowds that must be present during the academic year. The Classics Department was on the fourth floor of the Humanities and Social Sciences Building – a strange modernist structure, built like a triangle with a courtyard in the center.

They climbed the stairs and walked down the main hallway. The doors to almost all of the faculty offices were closed, but the main office was open and brightly lit. On the wall was a poster of the Acropolis, with ATHENS across the bottom in big black letters, but the office seemed to be deserted until suddenly a door to an inner office opened and a striking woman emerged.

Jupiter was certain that it was Nikoleta Kyriaku – the woman he'd seen talking to Dr. Stonebridge in the photograph taken at Dimitri Dimitriou's party. Her dark curly hair was pinned up, but otherwise she looked very much the same – tall and beautiful, poised and elegant. She smiled warmly at the four of them and asked if she could help them.

"This is the Classics Department, right?" Pete said. "The other day we met – "

Jupiter coughed and shot Pete a look of such warning that he instantly stopped talking. Pete's friendliness was so great, Jupiter thought, that sometimes it led him to be indiscreet. Bob and Mallory looked a little surprised, but it was clear they weren't about to say anything.

"We were just wandering around, really," Jupiter said. "Is this where the English and History departments are?"

"History is here," Nikoleta Kyriaku said. "But English is in South Hall, where the Division of Humanities and Fine Arts is housed."

"That's odd," Mallory said. "I would have thought that that's where the Classics Department would be."

"I can see what you mean," Nikoleta Kyriaku said. "But because our faculty teach not only language and literature but also culture and archaeology, we actually fit better here."

"Oh, right," Jupiter said. He was beginning to hatch a plan. His impulse to come to the Classics Department this morning had not been based on the thought that they might meet Nikoleta Kyriaku, but now that she had appeared, it only made sense to find out – if he could – whether she was related to the man who managed the store where Mallory had discovered the Greek coin.

He had long ago learned that, as an investigator, it was important to find the connections between people and to follow those connections wherever they led, and as a child actor, Jupiter had learned a few things that had become useful as he'd grown up. One of those was that if he acted a lot less smart than he really was, he could often get people to tell him things they otherwise wouldn't. He let his body go a bit slack; he loosened his cheek muscles and widened his eyes. This was what he thought of as his stupid face. He glanced at Bob, Mallory, and Pete to make sure they understood what he was about to do.

Now he stared in apparent wonder and amazement at the poster of the Acropolis.

"Do you have to be Greek to work in this department?" he asked.

Nikoleta laughed. "No," she said. "What gave you that idea? I don't think anyone who works here is Greek but me."

"Oh," Jupiter said. "You're Greek? Do you speak Greek?"

"Yes," Nikoleta said. "*Kalimera.* That means 'good morning.'"

"Wow!" Jupiter said. He pointed to the poster, with the word ATHENS in big black letters. "Are you from there?"

Nikoleta turned to see what Jupiter was pointing at. "No," she said, smiling. "Athens is the capital and on the mainland. Greece has many islands. I'm from one of them, in the Aegean Sea. It's called Naxos."

Jupiter smiled at her and nodded. For the moment that was enough. Nikoleta and Achilles shared the same last name, and both were from Naxos. While he would have to make certain, it seemed more and more likely they were related. He glanced at his watch.

"Gosh," he said. "We better get going. Our parents are going to be mad if we're not there when they come to pick us up. Thank you for being so nice to us."

"Yes, thank you," the others mumbled, turning to leave. Pete went first. Jupiter took up the rear. He glanced over his shoulder to see Nikoleta Kyriaku looking after them, a puzzled expression on her face.

"Gee, Jupe," Pete said. "What were you doing?"

"I was trying to ascertain her relationship to the man who manages Aegean Treasures," he said, "and I thought it would be rude to come right out and ask her."

"Rude," Mallory said, "and also ill-advised. Never tip your hand when you're investigating."

"You sound just like Jupiter!" Pete said, shaking his head.

While Jupiter didn't think that was *exactly* right, there was enough truth in it so that he smiled to himself. By now, it was later than he had planned, and they hurried back across the campus to find Rafael waiting for them in his truck − parked close to the residence hall where they were staying. This morning, at Mallory and Bob's insistence, Jupiter and Pete rode in the front of the truck, while Bob and Mallory climbed into the back.

The drive south to Santa Barbara went quickly, and soon Rafael was parking in front of a small but attractive house made of stone and shaded by two tall palms.

"How wild is that!" Pete said. "Dr. Stonebridge's house is made of stone. He even has a stone bridge!"

He did indeed, Jupiter noticed. It seemed like a bit of an affectation, since there was no water to be seen. They walked from the end of the driveway over the bridge and up the path to the front door.

Dr. Stonebridge came to the door as soon as they knocked, and he seemed very pleased that they were there.

"Come in, come in," he said. "So good to see you all again."

As he shook everyone's hand, Jupiter noticed again the silver bracelet he had seen at Isabella's. He was about to say something

about having seen a whole box of such bracelets at Aegean Treasures when Pete spoke first.
"Dr. Stonebridge," he said. "You actually have
a stone bridge!"

The professor laughed. "Yes, I do. You
boys have your question marks; I have my
bridge. It was a gift from my friend Dimitri
Dimitriou − half a joke and half a celebration
of the ancient Greeks' gifts to the world.
Dimitri marvels at all the things the Greeks bequeathed to us, and one of them was the
arched stone bridge."

"Rafael told me that the Greeks also invented libraries and theaters!" Pete said.

"The list is almost too long to remember," Dr. Stonebridge said. "I already told you
about the lighthouse. Did I mention the spiral
staircase? I like to think they came up with that
because they had stared long and hard at the
shell of a nautilus. They also invented the catapult, the waterwheel, plumbing, central heating
− not to mention democracy!"

"That *is* an impressive list of
achievements," Jupiter said.

"Indeed," Dr. Stonebridge said, "and
Dimitri doesn't want you to forget any of them.
He's woven as many of them as possible into
the design of his own home on the coast. It's a

truly interesting and curious place."

"Yes," Mallory said. "We've seen pictures."

"More research!" Dr. Stonebridge said. "Good for you! Did your research reveal that Dimitri built his estate around a cove that was supposedly once used by pirates and Spanish and Russian smugglers?"

"No," Mallory said. "But we saw a picture of a cave that was called a pirates' paradise."

"Wait a minute, wait a minute," Pete said. "Does your friend actually have a catapult?"

Dr. Stonebridge laughed. "No, young man. I'm sorry to say that is one thing his estate lacks." He paused for a moment and then went on. "The cove I was talking about is quite wonderful. There are a number of legends about it – for example, that the sand is finer and more sparkly, more mixed with quartz and silica, than the sand anywhere else on the coast around here. Allegedly the pirates and smugglers used the sand to polish their weapons and liked to bring their ships into the cove on the dark of the moon, because the beach shone faintly, even in the dark. But what am I doing? I've kept you standing out here far too long."

He led them through a living room with a fireplace and walls lined with bookcases stuffed with books and into his study at the back of the house. It was a cozy room, Jupiter thought, with a large desk on which a desktop computer sat. It was dimly lit; the drapes had been mostly closed against the heat, and the air conditioner was on. The floor was covered by one of the largest handmade rugs Jupiter had ever seen.

Mallory immediately commented on it.

"Thank you for noticing, my dear," Dr. Stonebridge said. "I quite love it. It's Turkish, made in Isparta, in the southwestern part of the country. Turkey, as you know, is very close to the Cyclades – the islands of which Naxos is one."

He had set up a number of folding chairs in a semicircle around his desk, and he invited everyone to sit as he took a seat in a large leather swivel chair.

"You're not the only ones who have been doing research," he said. "Since I met you the other day, I've had the opportunity to find your website and I've been doing some reading."

He looked at Bob, who, Jupiter could see, stiffened slightly. "Mr. Andrews, you are a fine writer and you have done an excellent job bringing your cases to life."

"Thank you, Dr. Stonebridge," Bob said, looking embarrassed but pleased.

The professor now looked at Jupiter. "I have to say that I'm very impressed with all your past successes, and sorry if I did not take you as seriously as I should have when first we met."

Jupiter said, "There was no reason why you should have."

"Oh yes, there was," said Dr. Stonebridge, now looking at Rafael regretfully. "A special apology to you, my friend. I should have known simply from your recommendation how good these young people are at what they do."

He sat back in his chair and put his fingers on his temples.

"I'm very grateful that you've come up to Santa Barbara, and that you hope to help me," he said. "Of course, I'm incredibly shaken by the theft of the Minoan Treasure – I feel as though it's a great personal loss. I certainly hope the police recover it soon. If not, it could lead to unpleasantness between the Greek and American governments, and it's a great embarrassment to the Museum of Classical Antiquities.

"Needless to say, I'm also disconcerted that the police seem to think I might have something to do with the theft, but that is such a ridiculous speculation that I'm sure they couldn't *really* believe such a thing. They just feel it's their responsibility to investigate all leads. We'll see what they say when they get here. But while we wait for them, I'm more than happy to answer any new questions you might have for me."

Jupiter could see that the professor was not taking the threat seriously enough, but for reasons he couldn't fully explain, he didn't begin by asking why the police might be interested in Dr. Stonebridge.

Instead, he mentioned that he and the others had been wandering around campus and had visited the Classics Department.

"My, my," the professor said. "It's very quiet over there at this time of year."

"Yes," Jupiter said. "It was quite deserted. But we did meet a Greek woman named Nikoleta Kyriaku while we were there. I couldn't help noticing that she was the same woman we saw standing next to you in a photo taken at Mr. Dimitriou's fundraising party. Are the two of you good friends?"

Dr. Stonebridge's cheeks grew slightly

pinker and he blinked a lot. Jupiter couldn't say that this had the suddenness and ferocity of Pete's blushes, but it was still a blush.

"Good friends?" Dr. Stonebridge said. "No, no, no, no, no. Ms. Kyriaku is a part-time secretary at the department, so of course I know her. But good friends?" He shook his head.

A child would have been suspicious of the speed and emphasis of Dr. Stonebridge's denial, Jupiter thought, even if the man hadn't blushed. What was he trying to hide? Jupiter decided to let the matter go for now, but not before asking one more question.

"Would you happen to know," he asked, "whether Ms. Kyriaku is related to Achilles Kyriaku, the man who manages Aegean Treasures for Mr. Dimitriou?"

Dr. Stonebridge looked vastly relieved that the questioning had moved on to safer ground.

"Yes," he said. "I believe Ms. Kyriaku is Achilles Kyriaku's sister. I seem to remember that, when we hired her, she mentioned that she also worked part-time as a clerk or cashier at a Greek store in Santa Barbara managed by her older brother. In fact, if I'm not mistaken, it was her brother who arranged for green cards both for her and for another brother when they first came to the United States."

"That's very interesting," Jupiter said. An idea was beginning to form in his mind, but it hadn't come to fruition before he began talking again.

"We actually stopped at the Santa Barbara branch of Aegean Treasures yesterday," Jupiter said, "on our way here. They sell all sorts of imported food and wine as well as touristy stuff. There was an entire barrel of reproductions of ancient Greek coins, and in it Mallory found − . Mallory, would you show Dr. Stonebridge what you found?"

Mallory had brought the paper bag with the five coins along with her in her backpack, and now she fished it out, rummaged in the bag, and handed Dr. Stonebridge the coin. He looked at it with curiosity, but in no time, his eyebrows shot up and his mouth fell open.

"Good God!" he said. "This is an authentic Alexander tetradrachm. It dates to the Hellenistic era of ancient Greece. What in the world was it doing in a box of novelty reproductions?" He looked genuinely baffled and confused to Jupiter. He really was an innocent, Jupiter thought.

"You told us yourself that coins like this

were lying everywhere all over Greece," Jupiter said, "and that anyone could find them."

"Yes," Dr. Stonebridge admitted. "That's true."

"We think that someone who works for Aegean Treasures," Mallory said, "– probably a number of someones – has been collecting them back in Greece and then smuggling them out of the country and into the United States disguised as reproductions."

"It's even possible that this is the twisted source of the rumors about you that Rafael was concerned about," Jupiter said.

"So you think this is why the police want to question me?" Dr. Stonebridge asked.

"We have no idea," Jupiter said, "but we do think we've uncovered a smuggling operation."

"This is terrible," Dr. Stonebridge said, visibly upset. "I'll have to tell Dimitri right away. After all, he owns the stores!" He reached for the telephone impulsively and then pulled his hand back. "In the heat of the moment, I forgot," he said. "Dimitri is in Greece now, for another week or so. I was actually hoping that word hadn't reached him about the theft of the Treasure, and that it would be rescued and returned to the Museum before he gets back from his trip."

This seemed to Jupiter like an overly-optimistic expectation. He was beginning to think that Dr. Stonebridge was indeed a bit like the old-fashioned stereotype of the idealistic, absent-minded professor – the scholar who lived in the fabled ivory tower and not in the world as it really was.

"I certainly hope the police find the treasure as quickly as possible," Jupiter said. "But I'm afraid you can't count on keeping the theft from your friend. I actually think it would be a good idea if you called him. Does he have a cellphone that you could reach him on in Greece?"

"By Jove," Dr. Stonebridge said. "I'll do it." He rifled through some papers on his desk until he found the number; then he pulled the landline toward him and dialed. Jupiter quickly calculated that it would be about ten o'clock at night in Greece. Dr. Stonebridge looked tense as the phone rang. Then his face relaxed. "Dimitri?" he said. "Is that you? It's Godwin calling from California."

Dr. Stonebridge did not put the call on speakerphone, so Jupiter had to deduce the conversation from Dr. Stonebridge's side of the conversation, and from the bits and scraps that he was repeating.

It turned out that Mr. Dimitriou had learned about the theft within an hour of its occurrence, and that he had been meaning to call Dr. Stonebridge for the past day. But he'd been insanely busy with other calls – he'd been in constant contact with the director of the Museum of Ancient Antiquities in Santa Barbara, with the Ministry of Culture in Athens, with the director of the archeological museum where the Treasure had been exhibited before it went to the United States, and also with U.S. Immigration and Customs Enforcement.

This last seemed to alarm Dr. Stonebridge until he was made to understand that ICE had a unit dedicated to the restoration of stolen or smuggled antiquities, and that they had already dedicated a veteran ICE employee to the case – a man named Hunter Baines, who had an excellent reputation.

"Yes, yes," Dr. Stonebridge said. "I'm sure you're right and that we'll get the Treasure back." He paused and smiled wanly at Jupiter and the others. "Yes, Dimitri. All those months on the dig on Crete, and the excitement of the find. Unearthing one piece after another. Yes, I'm sure you understand. But you're right – all that time and energy we spent convincing the

Ministry and the museum to lend us the pieces." He shook his head. "What an incredible blow."

And then he seemed to remember what had instigated the call. He sat up in his chair and looked straight at Jupiter.

"And I'm sorry to tell you there's more," he said. "I have some young friends with me – a group of young people called The Three Investigators and their Special Consultant. They investigate mysteries and are really very successful at it. They've just discovered an authentic Alexander tetradrachm in a bin of reproduction coins in your flagship shop here in Santa Barbara. They seem to think that an employee of yours – or several! – is using your operation to smuggle coins out of Greece and into the United States!"

He nodded several times as he listened to Dimitri Dimitriou, and then he shook his head, but whether it was in despair or disagreement Jupiter couldn't tell.

"And there's more," he said. "Apparently there are rumors on the Santa Barbara campus – and for all I know in town – that *I'm* the one smuggling antiquities out of Greece! Can you believe it? In fact yesterday after the robbery the police asked for a cheek swab to test my DNA! They want to interview me later this morning!"

Jupiter could see that the reality of the situation was beginning to set in. Dr. Stonebridge was looking more and more flustered and distraught. "Yes, thank you, Dimitri," he said. "I appreciate that very much. How long will you be? Three or four days still? Well, hopefully, all of this will be done and dusted by the time you get back to Santa Barbara. I certainly hope so!"

He tried to look cheerful but was having a hard time managing it. He shook his head. "No, no, I don't think there's any way for you to help. After all, you're – "

"Excuse me, Dr. Stonebridge," Jupiter said, interrupting the conversation. "There *is* a way that Mr. Dimitriou could help. Do you think he'd be willing to arrange for us to view the closed circuit TV footage that was taken during the robbery? Do you think he could ask the museum's director to arrange that?"

Dr. Stonebridge repeated the question and then nodded, listening. He smiled at Jupiter. "Thank you, Dimitri."

"And," Jupiter went on, "would he be willing to arrange an interview for us with Achilles Kyriaku, as soon as possible? Could he put us in touch with that ICE agent you mentioned earlier – Hunter Baines? We'd like to talk to him in person."

Dr. Stonebridge asked for the additional favors, then turned to Jupiter and asked him for The Three Investigators' e-mail address. Bob gave it to him and he told it to his friend. "Thank you, Dimitri," Dr. Stonebridge said. "You're a good friend and you've been most helpful. I – we – really appreciate it. Yes, you too. I'll look forward to seeing you next week." He hung up the phone and sat back in his chair, exhaling.

"He said he'll e-mail you the details of the various meetings as soon as he works them out."

"Thank you," Jupiter said. "That is most helpful."

Jupiter glanced out one of the study's windows that gave a view of the street. A police patrol car was driving slowly. It pulled to the side and parked a short distance from Dr. Stonebridge's house and two Santa Barbara policemen got out.

Looking at them, Jupiter got an uneasy feeling, and he turned to Dr. Stonebridge. "Could we have the coin back, please?"

Dr. Stonebridge handed it to Mallory,

who swiftly put it away in her backpack. "Not a word about the coin from anyone," Jupiter said. "Now let's go meet the police."

"Don't say anything, Godwin," Rafael counseled. "The police are not your friends."

"Don't be silly, Rafael," Dr. Stonebridge said. "I'm an open book."

That was just what Jupiter was afraid of, and as they walked toward the front door and the police, Jupiter's uneasy feeling just got more intense.

8

A Highly Upsetting Morning

Mallory's heart was pounding as she and the others walked through the house to meet the police in the driveway. Partly, she realized, that had to do with Jupiter's warning about the tetradrachm, which, even now, seemed to be sending out signals from her backpack. She had to assume that Jupiter feared the police would use it as more evidence against Dr. Stonebridge, no matter what the four of them might say. Or that they might simply seize it and not return it.

She was also worried about Dr. Stonebridge – who hardly seemed able to cope with what was happening. As their time with him had gone on, he'd seemed more and more jittery, and she had no idea what he might do when he was confronted by the police. Even now, he strode ahead, rushing into an uncertain future.

Once again, Mallory reflected that she didn't trust policemen at the best of times. Too many of them had become policemen in the first place because they liked the sense of power

158

it gave them, and she avoided people who liked having power over other people. She wanted to tell everyone to slow down, to wait for the police to knock, but before she could say a word, Dr. Stonebridge had opened the door and gone out to meet the policemen on the front lawn.

"Good morning, officers," he said heartily, as though they were old friends.

"Godwin," Rafael muttered to himself and the others. "Please be careful."

"Sir," one of the cops said, "are you Dr. Godwin Stonebridge?" His face was sunburned and beefy, and when he took off his hat, Mallory could see that his hair was thinning. He had a paunch and looked as though he wasn't very smart. His name tag read Office Reginald Reed.

"I am," Dr. Stonebridge affirmed. "What can I do for you?"

"We have a number of questions we'd like to ask you," the other cop said. He seemed sullen and angry, as though he resented having to do his job. He had bright blue eyes that looked to Mallory like cracked marbles. He had done a sloppy job of shaving that morning; Mallory saw he'd missed a patch on his left jawline. His name tag read Officer Johnny

Glass.

"Ask away," Dr. Stonebridge said brightly.

The sullen cop looked annoyed, as though Dr. Stonebridge's willingness to cooperate was making his job harder. "Can we go inside?" he asked. "I'd rather not ask the questions standing out here, if you don't mind. And can we lose the kiddie brigade? They'll only get in the way."

"What do you mean?" Dr. Stonebridge said, offended. "These are my friends."

"Friends or no," Officer Glass said. "They have no purpose here. We need to question you privately,"

"Excuse me, officer," Rafael said, stepping forward. "I'm Dr. Stonebridge's attorney, and these young people are my summer interns. They should definitely all be present for any questioning. It's part of their training, and you can't possibly have any objections. This is all very straightforward and casual, right?"

Glass looked carefully at Rafael, at his long hair and informal clothing, and he seemed both skeptical and suspicious. "You're his lawyer?" he asked.

Rafael nodded. Mallory could see that what had begun as a joke the night before had become serious business.

Before Glass could say anything further, Dr. Stonebridge said, "Why don't we all step inside? We can go back to my study where we won't be disturbed." Mallory wondered who in the world would disturb them, but she admired the professor's politeness.

There weren't enough chairs for everyone, so Mallory took a seat on the floor in the corner, instinctively keeping as much distance as possible between herself and the policemen. She was surprised when Pete joined her, grinning. Jupiter, Bob, Rafael, and the two cops sat in the folding chairs as Dr. Stonebridge sat down in the desk chair. At this point, he was holding his face in a fixed smile that looked as if it took a lot of effort.

As the questioning began, Mallory was glad she'd decided to sit on the floor. From her position, she could see everyone. The two policemen looked back and forth at one another as though they didn't know what to do next. To her surprise it was Dr. Stonebridge who asked the first question.

"Have you had any luck in tracking down the stolen items?" he asked. "It's been over twenty-four hours and I thought – "

"We don't know anything about that,"

Office Reed said. "We're beat cops. We just do what we're told."

"So neither of you is a detective?" Rafael asked.

Glass shook his head and pointed to his name badge. "Just 'officer,' like it says. I wouldn't get my hopes up about that jewelry."

"What do you mean?" Dr. Stonebridge said, aghast. "Aren't you doing everything you can to find it?"

"We're looking," Reed said. Though it was cool in the study, he kept mopping his brow with a pocket handkerchief. "But that stuff's tiny and it's made of gold. It could be in someone's pocket for all we know. Or melted down."

"Oh, no!" Dr. Stonebridge almost moaned.

"Don't listen to him, Godwin," Rafael said. "I'm sure *that* isn't true. Whoever stole the Minoan Treasure didn't want the gold. They wanted the antiquities."

Dr. Stonebridge looked relieved at Rafael's reassurance.

Officer Glass glanced at his wristwatch. Rafael saw him, too. "Are you waiting for something?" he asked.

Glass looked annoyed and ignored him.

"O.K.," he said. "Here we go." He looked at a small notebook he'd retrieved from a pocket and then hard at Dr. Stonebridge. "Your name is Dr. Godwin Cuthbert Stonebridge," he said. "Is that correct?"

Dr. Stonebridge nodded. "That is correct," he said.

"And you teach in the Classics Department at the University? You're an archaeologist?"

"Yes," Dr. Stonebridge said. "I spend half of the year in Greece."

What was going on? Mallory wondered. They knew all this. Why were the asking these questions?

"And what is your interest in the stolen items?" Reed asked.

"I discovered them!" Stonebridge said. "Years ago! And I helped arrange for them to be lent to the Museum of Antiquities."

They were stalling for time, Mallory thought, but she didn't know why.

"Could you stick out your right arm, please?" Glass asked. "And roll up your sleeve?"

Dr. Stonebridge seemed stunned by the request, but he did as he'd been asked. On his wrist Mallory could see the silver bracelet he'd been wearing when they'd first met him, like the ones for sale at Aegean Treasures.

"Tell us about that bracelet," Glass said. "Where you got it, how long you've had it, how much it cost, why you wear it."

Dr. Stonebridge looked like a deer caught in the headlights. He hesitated and looked to Rafael for reassurance. "I – I." He started again. "I've had it for some time," he said.

Mallory could clearly see that Dr. Stonebridge was a terrible liar. His eyes darted around the room and his hand twitched.

"I don't really remember how long. I think I must have gotten it on Naxos, a Greek island I visit, when I was there several years ago for the summer. It must have been quite inexpensive. We archaeologists have to watch every penny, you know?" He smiled at the cops but they weren't having any of it.

"And why do you wear it?" Reed asked.

"Because – ," Stonebridge stuttered. "Because – it reminds me – of Greece." Even he could see how lame that sounded.

Beside her, Pete was burbling and bubbling. "Why is he saying all that?" Pete hissed. "He had to have gotten that at Mr. Dimitriou's store!"

"Shh," Mallory said. "Don't say anything. I agree with you, but it's not our business to help the police. Besides, if Dr. Stonebridge isn't telling the truth, he must have a good reason. We'll find out soon enough."

After all, she thought, the police were just fishing. They hadn't arrested the professor or read him his rights, so things were still pretty low-key. Besides, maybe he *was* telling the truth. Maybe he'd gotten it from the same place on Naxos that the buyers from Aegean Treasures had gotten the ones they'd imported. She and Pete didn't know for sure.

Just then, Officer Glass's cellphone sounded with the trumpet fanfare that preceded a horse race. He rushed to answer it. Everyone grew very still and silent. "I've got to take this," Glass said, stating the obvious. He touched the screen. "Glass," he said. "Yeah." He was silent, listening. Mallory's heart began pounding again. "Uh huh," Glass said. "Understood."

He ended the call, looking more certain of himself than he previously had. He stood and stowed his phone. Then in a low harsh voice he said, "Dr. Godwin Stonebridge, you're under arrest for the theft of the Minoan Treasure from the Museum of Classical Antiquities."

Dr. Stonebridge's mouth dropped open.

"What?" he said. "But you can't possibly – "

"Godwin," Rafael said, also rising. "Don't say a word."

Glass continued. "You have the right to remain silent. However, anything you do say may be used against you in a court of law."

Mallory knew this was the Miranda Warning that the Supreme Court had mandated must be read or repeated to anyone being arrested.

"You have the right to consult an attorney before talking further with us now or in the future," Glass continued. "If you don't have an attorney, one will be provided for you." He looked pointedly at Rafael. "If this man can be believed, you already have an attorney."

"Well," Dr. Stonebridge said, looking between Glass and Rafael. "I – "

"Do you understand?" Glass asked.

"Yes," Dr. Stonebridge said. He had become very pale. "But – "

"Godwin!" Rafael said.

"Knowing your rights, is there anything you would like to say at the present time?"

"I'm innocent!" Dr. Stonebridge sputtered.

"Please stand and put your hands behind your back," Reed said, taking out a pair of handcuffs, to Mallory's horror.

"Is this necessary?" Rafael said. "Clearly you can see he's not about to give you any trouble."

"By the book," Glass said. As Reed fastened the handcuffs on Dr. Stonebridge's wrists, the professor winced.

"Why in the world are you arresting me?" Dr. Stonebridge cried. "What's your evidence?"

Reed looked at Glass, unsure of what to say next. Glass sneered. "You dropped a silver bracelet at the scene of the crime," he said. "Identical to the one on your wrist. Did you buy them in bulk?"

"I most certainly did not," Dr. Stonebridge said indignantly.

"The DNA we took from you yesterday is a perfect match for the DNA we found on the bracelet left in the museum," Reed said.

"That's — that's impossible!" Dr. Stonebridge said.

Bob shot to his feet. "Dr. Stonebridge," he said. "Do you have two bracelets? Could someone have stolen the other one and left it at the scene?"

"No, no," Dr. Stonebridge said, his voice rising. "I only have one bracelet. I've only ever had one bracelet, and it's on my wrist right now. Why would I need two? How on earth could another bracelet with my DNA on it have been found in the museum? It's a total mystery to me."

"Come on, let's go," Glass said. "We're going to the station."

"But don't I get a phone call?" Dr. Stonebridge said. "Everyone always gets a phone call."

"You'll get yours," Reed said. "After we've officially booked you."

"What's going to happen to me?" Dr. Stonebridge exclaimed. "I'll lose my job! I'll lose everything!"

"Don't, Godwin," Rafael said. "We'll do whatever it takes to get you out of this."

"Don't worry?" Dr. Stonebridge said. "That might as well be one of the twelve labors of Hercules!"

Officer Reed took one arm and Officer Glass took the other. Together they marched Dr. Stonebridge back through his house and out the front door. Mallory was stunned by the swiftness with which everything had suddenly happened, and she could see that Jupiter, Pete, and Bob felt just as helpless as she did.

Reed opened the back door of the patrol

car, put his hand on top of Dr. Stonebridge's head, and began easing him down into the seat. As this was happening, Dr. Stonebridge called out, "Rafael, please call Dimitri and tell him what has happened."

"I will, Godwin," Rafael said. "And remember. Keep your mouth shut!"

The door closed and Dr. Stonebridge was lost behind smoked glass. The two cops got into the front seat and drove off.

"Come on," Rafael said to Mallory and the others. "There's no time to lose."

He hurried back through Stonebridge's house to his study where he picked up the receiver and hit Redial. Mallory felt her anxiety rise as the phone rang. Then Rafael stood straighter.

"Dimitri," Rafael said. "Is that you? This is Rafael Solares, a friend of Godwin Stonebridge's. We met at the fund-raising party for special education that you held at your estate? I'm calling with some bad news, I'm afraid."

He paused. "Yes," he said, "I know. I was here with Godwin when he called you. But since then there's been an unfortunate development. I'm afraid the police have arrested him." He nodded as he listened. "No, not for suspected smuggling. For the theft of the Minoan Treasure!"

He listened for a minute and smiled. "Thank you," Rafael said. "That would be great. Let me tell my friends."

He covered the receiver and told Mallory and the others that Dimitri Dimitriou would call his personal lawyer in Santa Barbara at once and instruct him to send the very best criminal lawyer he could find to the Santa Barbara police station.

"Wait," Jupiter said. "Please ask Mr. Dimitriou if there's anything he can do to speed up our getting permission to view the CCTV tapes at the museum. It's important that we know what the police know. With the new information we've just received about the silver bracelet, it's more important than ever. Can he call the director and arrange it? We also wanted him to arrange those interviews with Achilles Kyriaku and Hunter Baines."

"Sure, Jupiter," Rafael said. "I'll ask him." He unmasked the receiver. "Dimitri, I'm back," he said. "Sorry to keep you waiting." He asked again for the favors that Dr. Stonebridge had asked for earlier, saying he was sorry to ask again, but things had obviously gotten a good deal more urgent since the requests had first been made.

Mallory sat still, watching Rafael's face for any sign of how the conversation was going. It seemed that talking to Dimitri Dimitriou was actually reassuring Rafael, and Mallory could only imagine the gravity and seriousness of purpose that the older man was conveying. She didn't know if he had ever had any experiences like this before, but he was clearly a man of the world, and she knew, from what Dr. Stonebridge had told them that he was very loyal and good to his friends. Now it would be Dr. Stonebridge who benefited.

"Yes," Rafael was saying, as he scribbled something on a piece of paper. "Got it. Yes, I'll hold."

He turned to Jupiter, Pete, Mallory, and Bob. "He's calling the museum's director right now," he said. "And he just gave me the telephone number of his estate manager – a man named Stavros Economides. Mr. Dimitriou is so crazily busy that he asked that you or I contact Mr. Economides directly and ask him to set up the interviews. He said Mr. Economides would be happy to help. He's met Dr. Stonebridge."

He held up a finger in a warning sign that Mr. Dimitriou was back on the line.

"Yes, Dimitri," he said. "That's wonderful. Thank you." He was clearly coming to the end of the conversation. "I understand. Yes, I'll tell him. Thank you for everything. I'll keep you informed. Goodbye."

He put the receiver back in its cradle and looked right at Jupiter. "He managed to reach the director," he said. "Because of the theft, the museum is closed, but if you go there in two hours, the tech guy will meet you and bring you in a side door. Then you can see the tapes."

"That's excellent news," Jupiter said.

There was a sharp knock on the front door, which startled Mallory and certainly surprised the others. Rafael answered the door, with the four of them clustered behind him.

There was another patrol car, this time parked in Dr. Stonebridge's driveway, and two more uniformed policemen stood at the door, brandishing a piece of paper.

"Warrant to search the premises," the taller one said. He was wearing sunglasses and he thrust the paper at Rafael. Rafael examined it and stepped aside. The shorter one went first, his eyes darting to the left and right.

"If you don't mind my asking," Mallory said, "what is it you're looking for?"

"I do mind, young lady," the one with the sunglasses said. "We're simply looking."

Obviously the cops had the idea that Dr. Stonebridge not only had stolen the Minoan Treasure but then had been stupid enough to bring it home and hide it somewhere in the house. The idea almost made Mallory laugh. Did the police think everyone was an idiot? After all, even a naïf like Dr. Stonebridge would have come up with a better hiding place for the treasure.

The cops started in the living room, though they were hardly thorough. They opened drawers and looked behind books in the bookcase without putting them back. They rifled through papers in an Arts and Crafts sideboard.

They made their way around the house — to the kitchen, Dr. Stonebridge's bedroom, and finally his study. Though they didn't make a mess, exactly, they left everything less tidy than it had been before, and when they finally left, about a half hour later, empty-handed and disgruntled, the entire house radiated disarray.

"That was certainly unpleasant," Jupiter said.

"They even looked in the refrigerator!" Pete said. "I mean, who would hide gold jewelry in a refrigerator?"

"I can't believe they were even here," Mallory said. "Can you imagine how dumb a crook would have to be to hide what he'd stolen in his own house?"

"It *is* unlikely," Rafael said, "but it was a place to start."

"I'm afraid that if this is the way they're going about it, then Officers Reed and Glass may have been right when they suggested that the treasure wouldn't be easily or quickly found," Jupiter said.

"Come on," Rafael said, "let's straighten things up, and then I'll drive you to the museum so that you can take a look at those tapes. If there's time, maybe I can call the station to check on Godwin."

The five of them spread out and did the best they could to make the house look the way it had before the cops started disarranging it. Then they filed outside and over to the battered yellow truck as Rafael locked the door behind him.

They were quiet as they started toward the museum. It had been a sobering morning, Mallory reflected. Though they had known the police wanted to interview Dr. Stonebridge, they hadn't known that an arrest was imminent

– even though the police had requested a DNA sample the day before. She hoped the professor would follow Rafael's advice and say as little as possible, though she doubted he would. Once they got him alone, she was sure he would talk his head off.

But what could he say? Surely nothing that would incriminate him, since he was clearly utterly innocent. She just hoped he was smart enough to keep to himself the fact of the rumors about him that Rafael had heard.

"I don't know how the rest of you feel," Pete said, and Mallory expected he'd go on to say something about how upsetting the morning had been.

" – but I was thinking maybe we should get some lunch!" Pete said.

Mallory was so surprised that she started laughing, and Bob and Jupiter joined in.

"What's so funny?" Pete asked, offended.

"It's just that we can always count on you to bring us back to basics," Bob said. "Heck, yes. I'm starving."

They found a small sandwich place not far from the museum, with a lengthy menu of options and an outdoor courtyard next to a fountain where wire tables and chairs had been set up. As they settled down to wait for their food, Mallory closed her eyes and took a deep breath. Because of the fountain, the air was cool and filled with ozone. It felt good to relax.

She opened her eyes and glanced at Pete. When he saw that she was looking at him, he shook his head and made an exaggerated frowning face. Pete was almost always happy-go-lucky, but he didn't seem that way now. In fact she suddenly understood that he was at least as upset about what had happened to Dr. Stonebridge as she was!

9

On The Trail Of Nikoleta Kyriaku

When the server brought the drinks and sand-wiches, Pete found he wasn't as hungry as he'd thought he was. The sight of Dr. Stonebridge being handcuffed and led out of his own house and put into a police cruiser had shocked Pete and left him with a queasy stomach. Before today, Pete's experiences with the police had been pretty positive. The chief of police in Rocky Beach was a good, kind, and fair man who had taken an unusual interest in The Three Investigators.

In fact, after Chief Reynolds had seen how helpful they were in solving several cases, he'd made them unofficial deputies in the Rocky Beach Police Department. As well, he and Pete shared a passion for baseball; Chief Reynolds had been a star in high school and college until a freak accident had ended his playing career.

But Pete hadn't liked Officers Reed or Glass, or the two other cops who'd been sent to search Dr. Stonebridge's house. They'd seemed mean and condescending, and his memory of Officer Glass referring to the "kiddie brigade" still stung. They'd been brusque and dismissive with Dr. Stonebridge, treating him as though he were guilty even before he'd been officially booked.

Pete, Jupiter, and Bob had been brought up to believe that a policeman was your friend, but Pete could see that was clearly not always the case. It depended a great deal on who the person was before becoming a cop. He took a drink of his lemonade and picked at his sandwich.

"What's the matter, Pete?" Bob asked.

"I'm still not over seeing the cops treat Dr. Stonebridge the way they did," Pete said. "He's such a nice man, and he was so upset."

"But I thought you were so hungry," Bob said.

"Not so much," Pete said. "It's all well and good for the three of you to laugh at me for always being interested in food. But when I suggested we stop for lunch, it was because I thought that eating was a nice, normal thing to do and I was in the mood to do something nice and normal after what happened." He paused. "Besides, it's almost two o'clock in the afternoon."

Mallory looked embarrassed. "I'm sorry

I laughed at you, Pete. But laughing was a re-lief after all that tension."

Pete picked up his tunafish sandwich and took a bite. It was pretty good. "I can't get over all that stuff about the silver bracelet," he said. "The cops said that they found Dr. Stonebridge's DNA on the bracelet at the museum. That's pretty strange."

"It certainly is," Jupiter said. "DNA doesn't lie."

"But remember at Skeleton Island?" Pete said. "Chris Markos was arrested and taken to jail when the cops found his knife at the scene of the crime. But later on he was proven to be innocent! It's the same kind of evidence, isn't it?"

"Yes," Jupiter said. "Except for the DNA."

"Well," Pete said. "There has to be some explanation."

"I'm sure there is," Jupiter said, "especially since Dr. Stonebridge is obviously quite innocent. Someone has set him up. How, we don't yet know."

"It's amazing how easy it is for cops to get stuff wrong," Pete said, "and then we all believe it's true even when it's not. My dad still talks about Skeleton Island sometimes, and how he thought Chris must have been responsible for all the trouble on the island, just because the police had arrested him and put him in jail. He still feels bad and doesn't like to think about it."

"I haven't heard about this before," Mallory said. "Was Chris set up too?"

"Yes," Jupiter said. "It's always convenient if the real criminal can set up some innocent person to take the fall."

"You know," she said, "it's been twenty-four hours since Bob and Pete called Chris on Naxos. Maybe by now he's found out something interesting about Dimitri Dimitriou or the Kyriaku family, or even Dr. Stonebridge. If he has, I bet he's sent you an e-mail setting up another Skype call."

"That's true," Bob said. "The last time I checked was this morning when we were still in the dorm. I brought my laptop, but it doesn't say if this sandwich place has Wi-Fi we can use. I'm beginning to wish I had a smart phone. It'll be great when we can finally get them next summer. Or I can, anyway."

"There's no need to wait until next summer to check your e-mail," Rafael said. "Do you want to borrow my phone?"

"Gee, thanks, Rafael," Bob said. "That

would be great."

Pete got up and went to stand behind Bob's chair so he could see what Bob was doing. Bob reached across the table and took the phone Rafael was offering. Pete watched as Bob navigated to The Three Investigators' server, signed in, and scrolled down the list of new e-mails.

"What are all those?" Pete asked. "Do we generally get so many messages?"

"Unfortunately, yes," Bob said. "Almost all spam. But Mallory was right! Here's a new one from Chris."

"Read it to us," Jupiter suggested as Pete went back to his seat.

"O.K.," Bob said. "Here goes." He began reading.

"'Dear Bob, Pete, Jupiter, and Mallory,'" he said. "He put 'and Mallory' in parentheses."

"Go on," Mallory said.

"'I spent the last hours searching and asking questions,'" Bob read. "'I don't want to write down what I have found but I think you will be happy! Especially good information about the Kyriaku family! Very much, very interesting. I can talk again tonight if you will be able to make the call. I will wait for you. Your friend, Chris.'"

"Wow!" Pete said. "That sounds promising."

"But it's already almost midnight on Naxos," Bob said, glancing at his watch. "If we're going to call, we'd better do it soon."

"That creates a bit of a problem," Jupiter noted. "We're due at the museum to watch the CCTV tapes. We're going to have to break up into two groups. Bob, why don't you come with me and Rafael to the museum, and Pete and Mallory, maybe you can make the call."

"How will we do that?" Pete asked.

"The museum is a bit out of town," Rafael said. "In fact, it's not that far from the campus. I could swing by the dorm and drop you and Mallory off, then drive back to the museum with Bob and Jupiter. We might be a few minutes late for our appointment with the director, but that would be all."

"That's a great idea, Rafael," Pete said. "Let's do it!" He'd been looking forward to talking to Chris again, and he thought that Jupiter and Bob would be better equipped to look at the tapes. They'd know what to look for. But Mallory was actually the one who saw things most precisely and remembered them afterwards. Maybe she should go, too.

He said that to the others, but Mallory

quickly quashed the idea. "Thanks, Pete," she said. "That's good of you. But Jupiter won't miss a thing, and anyway, I'm looking forward to talking to Chris."

"O.K., then," Jupiter said. "It's decided. I think we have two strong teams."

They paid for their sandwiches, left a good tip, and then piled into Rafael's truck for the drive to the dormitory.

When they arrived, Bob asked Pete and Mallory if they knew how to make the Skype call.

"Sure," Mallory said. "I've Skyped with a few friends back in Scotland, so I shouldn't have any trouble. I've got my laptop. All I need is Chris's Skype handle."

"Great!" Bob said. "It's GreekDiver20."

"What's the 20 stand for?" Pete asked.

"I don't know," Bob said. "I guess there are a lot of Greek divers."

The drive back to the residence hall took less time than Pete had imagined it would. As Rafael turned around and sped off toward the Museum of Antiquities and the meeting with the director, Pete and Mallory dashed across the lawn and through the front entrance of the residence hall. Upstairs, they unlocked the door to their suite and went in.

It was bright in there – even a bit glarey with the afternoon sun – and Mallory asked Pete to pull the drapes so they could see the screen better. They settled down at the table in the living room, and Mallory set up the call. "You ready?" she asked, as she typed in Chris's handle.

"You bet!" Pete said.

The screen popped open with a picture of Chris. He was wearing a white t-shirt, which set off his olive skin darkened by the sun. He was smiling maniacally, as though he couldn't wait to start talking. "Hi, guys," he said. "You got my e-mail!"

"Sorry we're calling so late," Pete said, "but it's been a busy day."

"For me too!" Chris said. "Where's Bob?"

"He and Jupiter are watching some closed-circuit TV tapes." Pete said. "We had two things to do at the same time."

Chris nodded and took a drink from a dark bottle.

"Hold on," Pete said. "What's that you're drinking?"

"Ginger beer," Chris said. "Very spicy. From Jamaica."

"You're drinking beer?" Pete asked.

"Does your dad know?"

Chris laughed. "It's not real beer. No alcohol. It's like a soda. Everyone is drinking it on Naxos this summer."

Part of Pete would have liked to just keep making pleasant chit-chat, but a bigger part of him knew that Chris might have found out something really useful − something that would shed a whole new light on the case. Maybe he'd discovered something that would help set Dr. Stonebridge free.

"O.K.," Pete said. "Let's get down to business. But first, I should catch you up. Over here, things have really gotten intense. Remember I told you that our new friend Dr. Stonebridge might be in trouble? Well, I got that right! The police just arrested him, and it's totally bogus. Again! Just like with you."

"I am sorry to hear that," Chris said, "but if anyone can clear him, it is you guys!"

"Did you have a chance to ask around?" Pete said. "What were you able to find out?"

"I talked to a lot of people about the Kyriakus," Chris said. "It's a big family. Two of the brothers own a construction business. With the new airport and all the hotels, they have been very busy for years. They are mostly boys, but there is one girl, named Nikoleta."

"We just met her this morning," Pete said.

"I told you last time about the oldest boy, Achilles, who saved the life of his friend Mr. Dimitriou. After he went to America, he brought over his sister and also one of his brothers to work for him in the store he manages. The brother's name is – "

He referred to a piece of paper on which he had taken notes.

"His name is Georgios," he said. "He did not have a good reputation on Naxos. Georgi is a thief and has been arrested. He was also accused of slapping a woman on the waterfront in Naxos Town. He went to jail for the thieving but not for the slapping, and because he had the criminal record he was not allowed to buy a metal detector. But he got one anyway."

"Wait a minute, wait a minute," Pete said. "Why couldn't he buy a metal detector?"

"People in Greece use them to search for buried treasure," Chris said, "and if you find anything, it is against the law to keep it."

"I think that's an unfair law," Mallory said, "making people give everything they find directly to the government."

"I do too!" Chris said. "But I cannot

change it. Anyway, in Greece if you see someone with a metal detector, you think the person
is searching for illegal treasure. So the government passed another law saying you cannot
buy a metal detector if you have a criminal
record."

"Wow!" Mallory said. "That's like guns
in America!"

"I know!" Chris said. "But you do not
hear of people shooting other people with metal
detectors! Still, the government thinks that if
you are a criminal, you will steal ancient treasures. And they are probably right!"

"So this Georgi got a metal detector,"
Pete said, "that he wasn't supposed to have?"

"Yes," Chris said. "And many people are
saying that he used it to look for ancient Greek
coins. They also say that two more of the
brothers – Panos and Antreas, who own the
construction operation – have made a lot of
money illegally selling pieces of ancient treasure. But none of this was ever proved."

"That makes sense," Mallory said. "If
they have heavy earth-moving equipment and
they dig big holes for the footings of buildings,
who knows what they might have found? What
a racket!"

"Yes," Chris said. "They have been

questioned by the Ministry of Culture and by the local police, but they have never been caught."

"Still," Pete said, "people seem to think these brothers are shady."

"Yes," Chris said. "But there are some Kyriakus who have good reputations. One of them is the chef at a restaurant on the waterfront who everyone thinks is great."

"What about the sister, Nikoleta?" Mallory asked.

"She has not been in trouble with the police," Chris said. "At least I could not find out anything about that. But I did hear an interesting story. I was told by a neighbor of hers that ever since she was a young girl, she was in love with a boy who was five or six years older than she was."

"In love?" Mallory asked.

"I do not know when this started," Chris said. "Maybe when she was a teenager or a little younger. Maybe she just had a – how do you say in English? A crutch?"

"I think you mean 'a crush'," Pete said, suddenly feeling a little weird. After all, he himself might be accused of having a crush on Califia, but when somebody else was having one, it sounded a little stupid.

"Yes!" Chris said. "That is what I mean. So she started liking this boy and then it turned into a crush and it didn't go away."

"Are you saying that she became obsessed with this guy?" Mallory asked.

"Sort of," Chris said. "Anyway, the boy she had a crush on went out with someone else who was his age – a beautiful girl – and he married her. They moved to Athens where he got a job working for the Ministry of Culture. Everything was very good for them, but she went out sailing and a squall blew up and she drowned. It was very sad, everyone says. So his friend from when he was a boy, Dimitri Dimitriou, brought him to California to manage his house and grounds."

"The estate manager!" Mallory said. "Stavros Economides!"

"Yes! That is his name," Chris said. "The people I talked to told me that Nikoleta Kyriaku wanted to go to California not to work for her brother but to be close to Stavros Economides."

"Did you find out anything about him?" Mallory asked.

"There were rumors that he did not leave Greece just because his wife had died," Chris said. "When he worked for the Ministry of Culture, an ancient stone statue of Apollo – a kouros – was discovered on Naxos. The government had claimed it, of course. But it disappeared on the way to Athens, and people whispered that Economides had something to do with that.”

“Wow!” Pete said. “Did Mr. Dimitriou know?”

“I do not think so,” Chris said. “Nothing was ever proven, but when Mr. Economides's wife died and then he was offered the job in America, it was quite convenient for him. He left the Ministry before anyone could look too closely at what he had done.”

“You did an awesome job, Chris,” Pete said.

“Really?” Chris said, beaming.

“Really!” Pete said. “I wish I was there so I could slap you five.”

All of a sudden, Chris's hand flew out and slapped the screen. “Ha ha!” he said.

“It’s great you were still up when we called,“ Pete said. “You must be pretty sleepy.”

“I was before,” Chris said. “But not now! I am wide awake from talking to you.”

“Get to bed, anyway,” Pete said. “We'll tell all this to Jupiter and Bob, and I'm sure Bob will write to you again soon. If we need to find out anything else, he'll tell you."

"You should come to Greece!" Chris said. "We would have fun!"

"Gosh," Pete said. "We'd love that. Bye for now."

Chris disappeared from the screen, and Mallory closed her browser and then the notebook itself.

"That guy is great," she said.

"I'll say!" Pete said. "And he sure found out a lot." As he was talking, he went to the windows to draw back the drapes and let the light in again.

Outside, on the lawn in front of the residence hall, Pete noticed a couple – a woman and a man – walking close together. The man had his arm bent and the woman had intertwined her arm with his and seemed to be leaning on his elbow. She looked familiar.

"Whoa!" he said, when it dawned on him who it was. "Come look at this! It's Nikoleta Kyriaku with some dude."

Mallory joined him and squinted against the afternoon sun. "That's her, all right," she said.

"Now I feel doubly bad for Dr. Stonebridge," Pete said. "He obviously had a crush on her, even though he didn't want to admit it, but the whole time it looks like she was into someone else."

"And not just anyone else," Mallory said. "You didn't see the pictures Jupiter and I saw of Dimitri Dimitriou's fund-raising party." She pointed. "Unless I'm very much mistaken, that's his estate manager, Stavros Economides. It looks like the rumors Chris heard back on Naxos are true."

That made sense, but Pete was still surprised. "What should we do?" he asked.

"You keep your eye on them while I pack up my laptop and grab my phone," Mallory said. "Then we should go outside and spy on them."

"Spy on them?" Pete said.

"You know, Mallory said. "Eavesdrop. The way we did when we followed Jack Cutter around the last time we were up here in Santa Barbara."

"Yes!" Pete said. "Surveillance. Let's do it."

Mallory jammed her laptop and phone into her backpack and threw it over her shoulder. Pete grabbed his backpack, too, and they rushed out of the room and down the corridor. As they left the building, the sun temporarily blinded Pete and he couldn't see anything at all.

But then he caught sight of the couple.

"Over there!" he said. They seemed to be walking toward a bus stop on the road between the dorm and the Pacific Ocean.

From what Pete could see, Nikoleta Kyriaku was over the moon. Whatever Stavros Economides said made her laugh. She walked close so that her shoulder rubbed his, and the smile on her face seemed to stretch from ear to ear. To Pete, Economides seemed a bit distracted. He kept looking around as though he was expecting something, and though he did not push Nikoleta away, he didn't draw her closer, either.

It was impossible to hear what the two of them were talking about because the wind off the water carried their words away. Besides, Mallory whispered to him that they shouldn't get too close lest Nikoleta see them and remember them from that morning. Not that she would think anything of that. But still, Mallory said, better not even to raise the question in her mind.

Pete was trying to look uninterested even as he strained to hear what they were saying when he noticed another man walking toward them. Right off, Pete could see that he was a bully to his bones – the type who hung around on the edges of football or rugby games, hoping for a fight to erupt, always ready to turn an argument physical. He was chunky, a bit overweight but well-muscled, with close set dark eyes and short hair in a buzz cut. He was the kind of guy Pete would normally cross the street to avoid.

But Nikoleta and Stavros knew him. As he approached, Nikoleta let go of Stavros and opened her arms to the newcomer. She pulled him close and kissed one cheek and then the other. Stavros looked grim but he shook the man's hand.

As he and Mallory watched, the three of them began talking. Pete still couldn't hear what they were saying, but he thought he caught the word "tonight," and the word "boat." Not that that was helpful in any way at all.

All of a sudden, Nikoleta and Stavros were kissing, a quick kiss, like a goodbye kiss, and then Stavros was walking away, back in the direction they'd come. Pete had no idea why he was doing this, but he wondered if Economides had parked his car somewhere and he was walking to retrieve it. Meanwhile Nikoleta and the other man were standing at the bus stop. Wherever they were going, it was

194

a different place from the one to which Economides was headed at the moment.

"It looks like the two of them are waiting for the bus," Pete said. Then over Mallory's shoulder he saw the bus approaching.

"Uh oh," he said. "Here it comes. What do you want to do?"

"I don't know," Mallory said. "What do you think?"

"I think we should get on this bus and follow those guys," Pete said. "I love surveillance. That's the best part of investigating, as far as I'm concerned – other than finding hidden treasure!"

"O.K.," Mallory said, nodding. "I'm game."

Pete and Mallory started sauntering toward the bus stop just as the bus pulled in. They picked up the pace and stepped up the stairs not long after the two they were following had boarded.

Nikoleta and the man with the buzz cut had taken a seat about halfway back – Nikoleta next to the window – and Pete averted his face and hurried past them, followed by Mallory. The bus was mostly empty, though he had to think it would soon fill up. So best to stay close to the quarry, if not too close. He opted for the second seat back from them and slid in, with Mallory close behind.

"Why are we doing this again?" Pete asked, nudging Mallory and smiling a little.

"I don't know," Mallory said. "But I'm glad we are. If they'd only talk louder."

They both leaned forward to get as close as they could to Nikoleta and the man she was with as the bus lurched forward, toward the Henley Gate.

"Here we go," Pete said, but after he had said it, he realized he didn't have a clue where the bus was headed. Nevertheless, he and Mallory were two detectives, following a lead, shadowing two suspects. He was proud of having suggested they do this, and he couldn't wait to tell Jupiter and Bob that he and Mallory had discovered something important!

10

Jupiter Starts To Crack The Case

As Rafael drove away from the residence hall after letting out Mallory and Pete, Jupiter regretted not being able to take part in the phone call with Chris Markos. At the same time he looked forward to what he'd discover at the Museum of Antiquities. Not for the first time, he wished he could be in two places at the same time, but the laws of physics rendered that impossible.

Pete and Mallory would report the facts of what Chris said, but there was so much more to a conversation – the tone of voice, the exact words used, the body language. Oh, well, he thought. In this particular context those things were probably not that important.

"Here you are," Rafael said as he pulled up to the curb. He pointed to the side of the museum. "That's the door I think you're supposed to use."

"Aren't you coming?" Bob asked.

"No," Rafael said. "I think I'll stay with the truck. If I go, I'll disrupt the balance. After all, half the advantage of being who you guys *are* vanishes the minute you appear with an adult."

As he and Bob walked across the grass toward the door Rafael had pointed out, Jupiter thought that Rafael's decision was both very smart and very considerate.

The door was locked, as he expected, so Jupiter knocked on the glass panels at the top and then watched through the glass as a figure approached. He unlocked the door and opened it just enough to stick his head out.

"The Three Investigators?" he said. "I've been waiting for you."

"That's us," Jupiter said. "Or rather two of us. I'm Jupiter Jones and this is Bob Andrews. Our friend is off making a phone call. Are you the IT guy?"

"That's me," the man said, smiling. "Stan Bloomberg." He looked to Jupiter as though he was in his late 20s. He had long brown-blond hair, a scruffy goatee, and a silver ring in his pierced ear.

"Dr. Dare is expecting you. He's with someone now, so he asked me to meet you and bring you to his office. Follow me."

The corridor was warmly lit from small spotlights in the ceiling. They went up a short flight of stairs and into one of the museum's galleries.

Because the place was closed, all the exhibit lights had been turned off, but the large marble statues on display seemed to glow with a cold dim light. Bob stopped in front of a statue of a seated female figure, her braided hair wrapped around her head. She was holding a scroll and a set of tablets.

Bob seemed lost in thought, reading the placard in front of the statue, until Jupiter spoke to him and he shook his head as though coming out of a trance.

"What was that?" Jupiter asked.

"Nothing," Bob said. "I'll tell you later."

They passed glass display cases holding pottery shards, several intact bowls, and objects made of clay and stone. Jupiter could only glance at them, but he, too, stopped before a Roman statue of Aphrodite, from the second century B.C.E. She was over six feet high and was missing most of an arm and part of a hand, but she still had her head, unlike many of the other statues.

Jupiter couldn't help but think of the conversation Bob and Pete and Mallory had had in Rafael's truck after they left Aegean Treasures – about Califia playing the role of Aphrodite in a play about the Greek gods. If

Pete had been here, Jupiter would have shown him the statue.

"Where was the Minoan Treasure displayed?" he asked Stan.

"In the Special Collections Room at the back of the museum," Stan said. "There's not a lot to look at now except a bunch of shattered glass. The police have cordoned off the room with that yellow police tape but I can take you back to see it after we look at the CCTV footage."

Jupiter and Bob followed him through a side door and down a short hallway of offices. One door, halfway down, stood open and light poured into the corridor. As they entered the room a pleasant-looking man stood up from behind his desk. He was medium-height, reddish-blond, ruddy-cheeked, and slightly overweight. The nameplate on his desk read KENNETH DARE.

"Dr. Dare," Stan said. "This is Jupiter Jones and Bob Andrews."

"Hello," Dr. Dare said. "Mr. Dimitriou said to expect you."

There was another man in the office. He remained seated, semi-slouched in an easy chair, his long legs stretched in front of him, his hands in his pockets. He wore a blue jacket and a tie, which had been loosened at the neck and spread sideways across his shirt like a slash. On his hip was an ICE badge.

He looked thin to Jupiter — almost gaunt — the skin of his cheeks stretched taut over his cheekbones, making him look slightly cadaverous. He was clearly very tall — Jupiter judged him to be several inches over six feet. His lips were curled upwards in a sardonic smile as he looked at Jupiter and Bob.

"This is Hunter Baines," Dr. Dare said. "He's a federal agent with Immigration and Customs Enforcement. He's been assigned especially to the case and, I hope, will shortly be able to announce that the Minoan Treasure has been recovered and can be returned to us. He's quite experienced in this sort of thing and has been very reassuring."

Baines nodded at Jupiter curtly. He made no move to shake hands.

From the expression on Dr. Dare's face, Jupiter could see that he had great faith in Hunter Baines. "I hope you're right," he said to Dr. Dare.

He thought fleetingly of saying that Mr. Dimitriou had already told them about Baines — had, in fact, suggested they contact his estate manager to set up an interview with the man.

But Baines did not look like the sort who would be pleased to hear that a very rich man had suggested he give an interview to two fourteen-year-old boys.

He turned to Baines, smiling. "Good luck to you," he said.

Baines chuckled condescendingly. "I don't need luck," he said in a lazy growl.

That was all it took to convince Jupiter that it would not be wise to bring up a possible interview. Baines clearly had the same dismissive and patronizing attitude the policeman at Dr. Stonebridge's house had had – the one who had referred to the "kiddie brigade." He had no interest in what Jupiter and Bob were doing at the museum, and Jupiter had the sense that, if Baines *did* know, he wouldn't have been too happy about it.

Jupiter wished that everything had happened differently – that Dr. Dare had been alone, that they had approached Hunter Baines sometime after he had been contacted by Stavros Economides. But he would have to play the cards he'd been dealt. He suspected Baines wasn't about to do anything to help him and Bob; in fact, he didn't seem like the kind of guy interested in helping anyone but himself.

As he thought this, Jupiter felt vaguely

nervous, and when he saw a paperclip on the director's desk, he picked it up and fiddled with it, then shoved it, along with his hands, into his pockets.

But he calmed down when he remembered that all he really wanted was to view the CCTV footage – and that involved Stan Bloomberg, and neither Dr. Dare nor Hunter Baines.

"Well," he said to Dr. Dare. "There's no reason my friend and I should take up any more of your time, especially when you're talking to such a skilled investigator. As you know, we're here for a different reason."

He turned to Stan Bloomberg and gave him a suggestive look.

"Oh," Bloomberg said. "Sure! Let's go!"

He led them back out to the hallway and then down to its very end to a door with the sign CONTROL ROOM on it. "Make yourselves comfortable," he said, gesturing to a number of chairs that had been pulled up before a desk on which a large monitor sat. Next to it was a small keyboard with a panel of buttons.

"That Baines guy didn't give much away, did he?" Bob said. "He was pretty tight-lipped. Not to mention unfriendly."

"Definitely not the cuddly sort," Jupiter

said. "As well as smug." He turned to Stan. "What do you think he's going to do?"

Bloomberg snorted. "Not much," he said. "In my experience people who work for the government aren't generally good for anything. If you want my opinion, the guy's an ass."

Wow! Jupiter thought. Hunter Baines had really rubbed Stan the wrong way. "What did he do?" Jupiter asked.

"He wanted me to erase the footage," Stan said. "He told me he and the cops had seen everything they needed to see. I told him 'No way.'"

"That's unusual, isn't it?" Jupiter asked.

"Not really," Stan said. "Back before everything became digital, there was just a single surveillance tape, and the cops would routinely take it with them and keep it for as long as they wanted. Often it never got returned at all. But they can't do that any more.

"Anyway, just to be sure, I backed everything up. Even if it got wiped, there would still be a copy. I wasn't born yesterday. You can't trust cops or anyone who works for the government."

That might be a little extreme, Jupiter thought − though he understood the impulse.

But Stan was just getting started. As it turned out, he really, *really* didn't like Hunter Baines.

"He's totally full of himself," Stan said. "But I can tell you what *else* he's totally full of. He bragged about how much time he'd spent in Greece, how familiar he was with the culture and all the antiquities. Obviously he thought that because I'm an IT guy I'd spent my whole life in a dark room staring at a screen."

He started fiddling with buttons on the keyboard and a high-speed whirring noise filled the room, a computer disk being loaded.

"Well, he picked the wrong guy," Stan said. "I spent three months on a Greek island called Naxos, working on an archaeological dig as a grunt laborer. Amazing job, amazing place. I took a course at the university from this professor named Dr. Stonebridge – he's on the Board of Directors here at the museum – and he got me the gig."

It was obvious, Jupiter thought, that Stan had no idea of Dr. Stonebridge's arrest.

"If I hadn't already finished my IT major, I might have switched to Classics," Stan said. "I really liked the dig. Anyway, it all worked out because I got to work here, in the museum, in the end."

"That's great!" Bob said. "It would have been hard to find another job that merged those two interests."

But Stan still wasn't finished. It was clear he hadn't been able to gripe to his boss Dr. Dare, and his dislike of Baines had been eating away at him.

"What a jerk!" he said. "Baines went on about how he'd been all over Greece as a special guest with this big important friend of his from the Ministry of Culture – something about his training for his job with ICE. Impressive? I don't think so! With all those buried treasure laws, government workers in Greece are bullies, just like government workers anywhere. They love to boss you around. And from what Dr. Dare says, some of them get rich – though no one knows how."

Under other circumstances, Jupiter might have been glad that was the end of Stan's diatribe, but in this case it had certainly given him and Bob a lot of what might prove to be useful information about Hunter Baines.

"You ready?" Stan asked.

"Yes," Jupiter said. "Let's get started."

"O.K.," Stan said, "here we go. I put together a continuous run, from one camera to the next. Obviously there were different feeds in different rooms. But just so you know, there's no security camera at the museum entrance, outside, so there's no footage before the thieves were inside."

"Did you talk to the guards?" Jupiter said.

"No," Stan said, "not directly. But I know what happened. These two guys dressed as cops — wearing fake mustaches and beards and dark glasses and gloves — knocked on the doors. Which were locked, of course. When the security guards went out to meet them, the fake cops said a break-in had been reported."

"Dark glasses?" Bob asked. "In the middle of the night?"

"I *know*, right?" Stan said. "How could none of that tip off the guards? But they fell for it completely. The fake cops shoved guns in their ribs and cuffed their hands behind their backs. Then they put black balaclavas over their heads and ripped off their disguises from underneath. Here's where we pick them up."

Stan pushed another button and a grainy black and white image filled the screen in front of them. Jupiter saw four men, two of them handcuffed, and with guns pushing at their backs, and two of them wearing police uniforms, but also with black balaclavas over their heads. The thieves each carried a duffle bag as they roughly shoved the guards ahead of them toward a flight of stairs.

"They put their disguises in the duffels," Stan explained, "and then took the guards down those stairs. In the basement, they disarmed the alarm system − which meant that no alarms would go off when they smashed the glass cases. Then they gagged the guards and cuffed them to some water pipes. There are no cameras in the basement, so I'll skip ahead to − There."

The hooded men were now coming back up the stairs, and as they were facing the camera, Jupiter got his first real look at them. They seemed to pause so that whoever was watching could get a good look, as though they were taunting the viewer.

"Where's the central feed for the CCTV cameras?" Jupiter asked.

"In the basement," Stan said.

"You mean, they turned off the alarm system but left the surveillance system on?" Bob asked.

"Yes," Stan said. "Crazy, isn't it?"

"It's almost as though they wanted to be seen," Jupiter said. "As though they wanted a record of the robbery."

"It does seem that way," Stan said, "but it doesn't make much sense to me. I mean, they're totally disguised with the uniforms and the balaclavas. Maybe they couldn't find the feed?"

"Does that seem possible to you?" Jupiter asked.

"Not really," Stan said.

Jupiter watched as the thieves sauntered through the museum, the beams of their flashlights darting here and there, momentarily lighting up a statue before moving on. They didn't pause for a second; they knew what they were after, and they were on their way to get it. As they moved, Jupiter realized that there was one thing that the uniforms and balaclavas could not disguise – the thieves' basic body types.

One of them was an ectomorph – tall and slender, with narrow shoulders and long arms and legs. The other was a mesomorph, with a more athletic build, less tall, broader shoulders.

From what Jupiter could see, the tall one looked a lot like Dr. Stonebridge. A whole lot.

He looked more closely. Could Dr. Stonebridge have been acting as though he were innocent, when he was really guilty?

"Did you know the police have arrested Dr. Stonebridge?" Jupiter asked Stan.

Stan was shocked and astonished. "No!" he said. "That's nuts!"

Jupiter pointed to the screen. "The tall guy looks like him," he said. "It looks like they found an operative with the same body type so they'd have an easier time pinning it on the professor. Could you stop the feed so I can study the two men?"

Stan pressed a button and the frame froze, with the men in mid-step. Jupiter studied the width and slope of their shoulders, the position of their arms, the way they held their bodies. Dr. Stonebridge was a humble man, and his body radiated openness and a certain self-effacement. These two were confident, even arrogant.

"They sure seem to know where they're going," Bob said. "Why do you think they didn't take anything else?"

"It was actually a pretty smart move," Stan observed. "Most of the stuff in the museum is incredibly heavy. Even the smaller pieces are mostly stone or bronze or very fragile. The total weight of everything they took — the whole Minoan Treasure — is about fifty pounds, and as you'll see, they split up the loot between the two duffel bags. They were traveling light."

"Did you know," Jupiter asked, "that this seems to be a copycat heist, based on one from the Isabella Stewart Gardner Museum in Boston?"

"Yeah," Stan said. "We were talking about that earlier. I hope it goes down better here. The Gardner still hasn't gotten its stuff back, and it's been over thirty years. The $10 million reward for information still stands. I feel sorry for the people at the Gardner."

"It's like the paintings were stolen from all of us," Bob said. "All you had to do in order to see them was to go to the museum. And what have the thieves been doing with the stuff for thirty years? What do you *do* with a stolen painting?"

"Good question," Stan said. "Not as easy to unload it as you might think. Sometimes the thieves offer to return the stolen stuff for a ransom. It's cheaper for the museum and the insurance company to pay a relatively small amount to get them back, rather than to suffer the loss of the huge amount the work was worth."

"It's sort of surprising the thieves didn't do that with the Gardner," Jupiter said, "considering the value of the reward just for information."

"Yeah," Stan said. "That would be a lot less trouble. But sometimes – at least with paintings – the thieves pretend that what they're selling is a very high-quality forgery and they offer it for maybe 10% of what the painting is actually worth," said Stan. "So then it's hanging on someone's wall somewhere, and the new owner has no idea it's the original."

"Hiding in plain sight," Jupiter said. "But we have a friend who might be able to tell the difference. Maybe not with paintings, but with other sorts of artifacts, she seems to instinctively know if something is authentic." As he said this, Jupiter remembered how proud he had felt of Mallory for having discovered the authentic Alexander tetradrachm. Maybe *she* should have come with him, and Pete and Bob should have called Chris.

"That's a great skill," Stan said. "She's got a career path if she wants it." He squinted at Jupiter and Bob, then continued with his explanation.

"And sometimes the stolen stuff just completely vanishes. There's a theory some of it winds up in the hands of unscrupulous collectors who can never show it off or sell it, but who just want it anyway because they love it. And one of the reasons they love it is because no one else can see it."

"That's pretty perverse," Bob said.

"But really none of that applies to the pieces that were stolen in this theft," said Jupiter. "When it comes to stolen or illegally exported antiquities, there's rarely a history and certainly no 'signature,' so I would assume it's safer to acquire. Could you start the tape again?"

Stan hit a button, and Jupiter watched as the two men approached a set of doors with the words SPECIAL COLLECTIONS in gilt letters above them. The men threw open the doors, took heavy hammers with oversized heads from the duffels, and approached the first of the glass cases that held the Minoan Treasure. As the tall one hoisted the hammer overhead, ready to break the glass, his wrist thrust upward and Jupiter saw a glint of metal.

"Wait," he yelled. "Pause, please." When Stan did that, Jupiter asked if he could isolate the wrist with the hammer and then enlarge it.

"Whoa!" Bob said. Jupiter nodded grimly. On the outstretched wrist was a silver bracelet with engraved letters, apparently identical to the one that Dr. Stonebridge wore. But something about it seemed a little different to Jupiter.

"That's Dr. Stonebridge's bracelet!" Bob said.

"Correction," Jupiter said. "That looks like Dr. Stonebridge's bracelet. Maybe this is the real reason the thieves didn't cut the cameras. They wanted to be sure that we saw a picture of one of the thieves wearing the bracelet that he was later going to leave inside the shattered case."

"Wow," Bob said, "That's devious."

"And cunning," Jupiter said. "After all, the one he's wearing has to be bracelet #3. Obviously the thief can't have worn the one that shows up in the case. That one has Dr. Stonebridge's DNA on it. I don't know how they managed to engineer that, but I suspect the thief has it stowed in a plastic bag in one of his pockets. All right, Stan. Let's watch the mayhem."

The footage started again and Jupiter was shocked by the savagery of the hammer descending on the case holding part of the Minoan Treasure. Off to the left, the other thief was smashing the top of another display case.

Fragments of glass exploded upward

and in every direction. Once the initial breach had been made, the thieves tapped with the hammers and then pulled pieces of glass up and away from the case, to keep the ancient artifacts safe. Then, carefully and methodically, they took small zip-lock plastic bags and light-weight cardboard boxes from the duffels and into each one they put a separate piece of gold jewelry.

"It's good to see they're not harming the individual pieces," Bob said. "And the packaging would have kept the treasure safe if the pieces jostled against one another."

"They're protecting their investment," Jupiter said.

He watched as the two thieves got down on all fours, blocking their hands and the fronts of their bodies from the camera with their torsos.

They seemed to be brushing through the glass rubble, but Jupiter suspected it was a distraction of some sort. They got to their feet and whisked through the broken glass inside the main display case, as though making sure they hadn't missed anything. Shards of glass flew out and landed on the floor.

Then they stepped back, seemingly in a hurry, and there amid the debris, Jupiter caught sight of a glint of metal on the bottom of the case. Stan froze the image and enlarged it. Sure enough, there was a replica of Dr. Stonebridge's bracelet. The tall thief must have managed to take the one off his wrist and hide it somewhere while he took the other one with Dr. Stonebridge's DNA out of safe hiding and put it in the case.

The entire switch had been done rather well, Jupiter thought, seamlessly, fluidly, and quickly. Nevertheless, he thought the thieves were rather bold in their assumption that the police would believe the bracelet could have fallen off the wrist of the tall thief without him noticing it. The whole thing was obviously an elaborate set-up.

To Jupiter's satisfaction, when the footage resumed, the tall man seemed to hold his wrist up to the camera, as if to demonstrate that the bracelet was no longer there. The man's wrist was perfectly ordinary, though Jupiter saw that the wristbone protruded noticeably, and there was a triangle of three large freckles next to it. The man stood beside his partner in crime, and Jupiter suddenly noticed that the mesomorph was looking right at the camera. "Hold it," he said, and Stan froze the frame.

"Could you do a close-up on the face of the shorter guy?" Jupiter asked. When Stan did, Jupiter found it unnerving to stare directly into those two cold eyes, dark and flat – the eyes of a predator who obviously didn't care who was watching.

Then Jupiter saw something that made his heart leap. A real clue. "Look at that!" he said excitedly. "Look at the guy's right eye. Do you see the little scar right under it?" It was just barely visible through the slit in the balaclava.

"Yes," Bob said. "Good catch, Jupe!"

When Stan started up again, Jupiter watched as the two men unhurriedly picked up the two duffels and left Special Collections.

"That's about it," Stan said. He pushed a button and the camera froze on the crime scene, glass everywhere. "If you want I can let you see them walk out of the museum, but that's all that happens, and there are no close-ups."

"That's fine," Jupiter said. "Thanks for showing it to us – and also for putting it all together the way you did." He was pleased with how much the tapes had managed to reveal, at least together with some serious thought and analysis – the men's body types, the ostentatious setting-up of Dr. Stonebridge, the tall man's wrist, the heavier man's scar.

Stan shut the system down. "My pleasure," he said. "You guys are great even though you're so young."

"How old do you think we are?" Jupiter asked.

"I don't know," Stan said. "Fifteen?"

"Actually we're in our early twenties," Jupiter said.

"Really?" Stan said, looking shocked.

"Only kidding," Bob said. "We're both fourteen."

"That's a relief," Stan said. "Come on. I'll take you to Special Collections."

Stan was adamant that they not cross the police tape, which was crisscrossed over the main door into the room, so Jupiter had to be content with seeing everything from a distance. There wasn't anything that struck him – nothing new – and besides, he'd seen a great deal on the tape.

Back in the director's office, Jupiter was pleased to find that Hunter Baines had left. He and Bob thanked the director for his help and cooperation.

Stan walked them to the door where he'd met them.

"Thanks a lot, Stan," Bob said. "You

were great."

"Yes," Jupiter said. "Thank you."

"Gentlemen," Stan said, clicking his heels together. "It's been an honor. And listen – if you need any specialized help in the future, you know where to find me."

Jupiter and Bob left by the side door and joined Rafael. He was under a nearby tree, in the shade, his back against the trunk, reading. "How did it go?" he asked.

"Very well," Jupiter said. "I'll fill you in on what we learned. The short version is that the thieves went to a lot of trouble to set up Dr. Stoncbridge."

Two hours had passed since they'd left Pete and Mallory at the dorm, and Jupiter thought that they would long since have finished their talk with Chris. But Bob's cellphone hadn't rung. Jupiter wondered why Mallory hadn't called to let them know they were done.

As they climbed up into the cab beside Rafael, Jupiter said, "Bob, why don't you give Mallory a call? She and Pete can't still be talking to Chris, can they?"

"Seems unlikely," Bob said. "We only talked for about a half hour the first time. Of course, Chris would want to report everything he'd learned."

"If they're done, we can pick them up, and then, hopefully, we can all go out to Mr. Dimitriou's place. Maybe Mr. Economides can arrange for that interview with Achilles Kyriaku. I've more or less given up on Hunter Baines."

"Why?" Rafael asked.

"We just met him," Jupiter said. "He's not going to be helpful."

Bob pulled out his cellphone as Rafael drove away from the curb and started heading back in the direction of campus. He looked at Jupiter, a puzzled expression on his face, and shook his head. "Nothing," he said. "Should I leave a message?"

Jupiter shook his head and pinched his lower lip. This was strange, he thought.

"I wonder why Mallory's not answering?" he said, suddenly feeling a little worried.

11

To The End of the Line

As the bus passed under the Henley Gate and started toward wherever it was going, Mallory glanced back toward the dormitory she and Pete had just left. It had been a bit odd being there with just Pete for company – but less odd than she would have thought beforehand. Although this was the first Away case – as opposed to a Home case! – on which she, Bob, Pete, and Jupiter were all staying in the same quarters, it was amazing how natural the whole thing seemed.

Of course, on the last case, in the Napa Valley, they'd all slept in nearby rooms at the Castello Serreno – but only on the last night. The summer before, they'd never stayed anywhere together – except in separate tents in Rafael and Elena's back yard.

It felt very cool to be functioning like a real team at last – though what felt even more important was that she and Jupiter had finally done research together, when they'd gone to the Rocky Beach library and found out everything they could about Dimitri Dimitriou. And not only that – together they'd come up with the probable reason the Alexander tetradrachm had been in the barrel of reproductions, and had later explained it, together, to the others.

That was a whole lot of togetherness, Mallory thought, smiling to herself – and the great thing was that it really seemed to be leading somewhere. She wondered what Jupiter and Bob were discovering at the museum and half-wished she was there.

As the bus rattled on, she decided she'd better come up with a cover story for what they were doing there. Nikoleta Kyriaku hadn't seen her or Pete yet, but if she did – and if she recognized them – Mallory wanted to be ready.

After all, it had only been that morning that Nikoleta had met them – along with Jupiter and Bob – at the Classics Department, and even forgetful people could keep a face in their memory for *that* long. When she and the boys had left the department, they'd told Nikoleta they were meeting their parents. For them to be parentless so many hours later might seem a bit suspicious.

Maybe they could say, if asked, that Mallory's and Pete's mothers had called and asked them to take the bus to meet them – so that's what they were doing. They were taking this bus to wherever it was going – because that was where their mothers were.

Mallory shook her head at how preposterous that sounded. It was hardly an airtight story. And since she knew nothing about Santa Barbara's bus routes, if Nikoleta asked follow-up questions, Mallory would be in hot water. But she consoled herself with the fact that she was generally over-prepared and that things rarely got as dire as she imagined they might.

And she was often lucky – as she was today, it seemed. On the side of the bus next to Pete was a map of the city's bus lines, with this bus's route mapped in red. She studied it and saw that if they just stayed put, they were headed for the far outskirts of Santa Barbara and close to the sea. If anyone – if Nikoleta – asked, she could say her mother was visiting a friend in that area and was going to pick up Mallory and Pete from there.

Now that she had a reasonable explanation, she settled down to business, straining to hear whatever it was that Nikoleta and her companion were saying. Pete sat next to her, leaning forward, tense with expectation. The man with Nikoleta had begun talking loudly but in a language other than English.

"Keep your voice down, Georgi," Nikoleta said, in English. "We're not the only people in the world who speak Greek, you big oaf." Though what she said was a bit harsh, her tone was kind.

"Sorry, Niki," the man said. "I forget."

"Better that we speak English," Nikoleta said. "You need to practice. And it will remind you that we have to speak very softly."

Mallory looked at Pete, who glanced at her, eyes wide. "That must be the brother Chris told us about!" he whispered.

Mallory nodded and put a finger to her lips. Then she turned back to listening.

"Is everything O.K. with — you know?" Georgi asked.

"Yes," Nikoleta said. "I think so."

"I still do not understand why you did not tell me before," he said. "I am good at this. I would have helped."

The bus came to a halt at a bus stop and two people got on with shopping bags. While they were being seated, Nikoleta and Georgi stopped talking and watched them.

Even after the bus had taken off again, with a belch of diesel smoke, they remained quiet, as though the stop had sapped them of energy. Out the window, Mallory saw signs for the Santa Barbara Airport and for Goleta

Beach Park and Goleta Pier. The bus headed southeast toward Santa Barbara proper. When they were well underway again, the conversation resumed.

"I know you would have helped," Nikoleta said, "but I didn't want to get you involved. Too risky." She paused. "And not just you. *I* didn't want to get involved either."

"But you *are* involved," Georgi said.

"Yes," Nikoleta said, with a heartfelt sigh.

There was only one thing that they could be talking about, Mallory thought. The idea that Nikoleta Kyriaku was partly responsible for the theft of the Minoan Treasure astonished her.

"This is big, Niki," Georgi said, "not like shoplifting."

"I do not do that any more," Nikoleta said, "and besides, this is a one-time deal. I'm not going to become a thief."

"I do not understand," Georgi said. As he returned to this point, Mallory could see he was becoming more upset. Nikoleta was trying both to soothe him and to calm him down. "Is it that you do not trust me?" Georgi asked, his tone almost plaintive.

Nikoleta reached out and punched his

shoulder lightly. "You know that is not true, little brother."

"I am not so sure," Georgi said. "When me and Panos and Antreas came up with the plan to bring the old coins over here, *I* trusted *you* to help us."

Pete glanced at Mallory and grinned.

"But that is different," Nikoleta said.

"How?" Georgi insisted. "How?" His voice was getting louder again.

"As you said," Nikoleta said. "This is big."

"You don't think bringing in the coins is big?" Georgi retorted. "You should know better than anyone how much money we have made."

"I did not mean big like that," Nikoleta said softly. "This is a robbery that will be in newspapers all over the world."

"Yes!" Georgi said. "So why not me?" He pounded his fists on his chest, aggrieved.

"Georgi! Calm down!" Nikoleta hissed. "You get so – I don't know how to say it." She reached out and stroked Georgi's cheek with her knuckles. "So excited, so loud, like you did just now. I trust you, but you cannot trust yourself."

Georgi seemed to deflate. He sat for a moment in silence and stared out the window, withdrawing.

"Georgi?" Nikoleta said.

"What you said is true," Georgi admitted. "The judge said I cannot control myself."

"That's it," Nikoleta said. "Impulse control. So I was just trying to keep you safe. Because I love you."

Mallory could see that Nikoleta must have spent much of her life trying to protect her younger brother from his own anger and idiocy. For whatever reason, he was sullen and surly and always getting into trouble. But in spite of Nikoleta's efforts, Georgi had wound up in jail. She might even have thought when they came to America she was getting him out of Greece for his own good.

"Still," Georgi said, puffing himself back up. "I would have been good." His tone was wistful. Mallory could see he clearly regretted not being allowed to commit mayhem.

"That is true," Nikoleta said. "But I did not want to take the chance. We could have a good life here."

"Does Achilles know?" Georgi asked.

This was something Mallory herself had wondered. Did he know about the coins? Was he in on it?

"About the treasure?" Nikoleta asked.

"Of course not. He will know nothing, so keep your mouth shut. He has had nothing to do with any of it − not the warehouse operation and not the gold, and it must stay that way so that he is protected." She shook her head. "I feel so bad about what we have done."

"I know," Georgi said. "He has been very good to us − bringing us here and giving us jobs. He has a very good nature and is very loyal to his family. Like you."

"So you feel bad too?" Nikoleta asked.

"No," Georgi said, smiling grimly. "A business like Achilles manages was too good to ignore."

"Maybe we stop soon?" Nikoleta asked.

"I do not think so," Georgi said. "So long as Panos and Antreas keep digging in the dirt with their big shovels and finding coins, they will keep sending them in the barrels with the fakes. It is a good − how you say?"

"Distribution of labor," Nikoleta said.

"Yes!" Georgi said. "They find the coins, I take the real ones out of the barrels, and you find people to sell them to."

So that was how it worked! Mallory thought. The scheme made sense − a closed circuit of Kyriaku siblings, held together by family loyalty. But Georgi was prone to mistakes. Mallory thrust her hand in her pocket and her fingers closed around the Alexander tetradrachm that Georgi had obviously missed.

"Yes," Nikoleta said, "but you must remember that there will not always be people who want to buy."

"Just so long as they do not run out before the coins run out," Georgi said.

The bus was not air-conditioned, and the air was stuffy. Clearly Nikoleta thought so too. She was fanning herself with her fingers. "Aren't you hot?" she asked Georgi.

He shrugged as though the temperature of the air was nothing he concerned himself with.

Nikoleta turned to the window next to her which had not yet been opened. She pinched the levers and tried to lower the top pane but it didn't budge.

"I can help," Georgi asked. He reached across his sister, grabbed the latches on her window, and tugged downward. The top pane screechily obeyed. He was *strong*, Mallory thought.

"Thanks," Nikoleta said. "I knew you were good for something." She laughed.

"Ho, ho!" Georgi said. "Efcharistó." He sat back in his seat.

"That must mean 'you're welcome,'" Pete whispered.

Nikoleta's attempt at a joke had reminded Georgi of his bruised ego, and in no time he was back to asking her why she hadn't wanted his help in stealing the Minoan Treasure.

"I told you before," Nikoleta said. "I didn't want to get involved myself. But I couldn't say no when Stavros asked me."

"Did he threaten you?" Georgi asked, instantly affronted.

"No, no, of course not," Nikoleta said. "You know I'm a total pushover when it comes to the men I love — in the family or out of it. When you asked me to help with the warehouse goods, I said yes, because it was you. And when Stavros asked for my help with the Minoan items I couldn't say no."

"You have been in love with him a long time," Georgi said, his voice tinged with wonder that such a thing might be possible.

"Yes," Nikoleta said. "Since I was fourteen. And when his wife died and I came to this country, I had a whole new chance. I have been so happy with him for the last six months. I only wish that it had not involved the professor."

Mallory sat up straighter and listened even more carefully. Beside her, Pete bristled with attention.

"He has been very good to me ever since I started working at the university," Nikoleta continued. "He is a very nice man. Always treats everyone with kindness and respect. From the student workers to the cleaning people to the staff to his colleagues, always the same. Not like most of the professors who are so snooty if you do not belong to their club."

"What is his name again?" Georgi asked.

"Dr. Stonebridge," Nikoleta said. "He has a crush on me."

Pete looked at Mallory and shook his head in dismay.

"You are a beautiful woman," Georgi said. "He has good taste."

"He is a baby," Nikoleta said. "I do not know if he has ever been with a woman before. But I have felt so badly about what I did, and now he has been arrested."

"Better him than Stavros," Georgi said. "No?"

"That is what Stavros thought, and why he pushed me so hard," Nikoleta said. "It was Stavros's idea, the bracelet."

Mallory thought back to the visit to Aegean Treasures and the tray of silver bracelets with the machine for stamping initials.

"I cannot believe he wore that flimsy thing. Doesn't he always wear a jacket and tie?" Georgi said.

"I told you he has a crush," Nikoleta said. "Which is what Stavros was counting on."

"It must have been a good plan," Georgi said.

"Again, Stavros," Nikoleta said. "He is very smart. When I first gave the bracelet to the professor, he asked me out for a cup of coffee, but I said no, and kept saying no – I had many excuses. Then last week he went to a place south of here where he gave a lecture or workshop. When he came back, Stavros's plan was ready so he said I should say yes.

"We were sitting in a booth at Café Joe and he was being very embarrassing, thanking me again for that cheap little bracelet. I asked him if I could see it, and he slipped it off his wrist and handed it to me. I fumbled it in my lap and switched it with the other one I had brought, and then I put the one he had been wearing into a plastic bag to keep it safe and put that into my purse. This was not good of me, and I am sorry about it."

"He did not notice?" Georgi asked.

"Why would he?" Nikoleta said. "They are exactly the same. I had both stamped with the same initials, and I put the new one down on the table so it would have cooled from the heat of his wrist. And then that night I gave the one in the plastic bag to Stavros. I do not know what he did with it. I did not want to know all the details, and he did not tell me. But I know that Dr. Stonebridge was arrested today, and I am afraid it is partly my fault."

"So you didn't do too much?" Georgi asked. "Just that, with the bracelet?" Nikoleta nodded. "Still, you were wrong not to tell me. I am excellent with the smash and grab. But it's too late now. Anyway, look on the bright side. Everything's going good with the coins and our own operation. Here's my stop. I've got to work."

For some time now, the bus had been moving through the streets of Santa Barbara proper, past restaurants and dry cleaners and grocery stores and corner stores. Mallory noticed that the street the bus was on looked familiar and then she saw why. They were just down the block from Aegean Treasures.

The exit doors in the middle of the bus opened, and in no time Georgi was walking down the street toward the storefront. Pete and Mallory stayed seated two seats behind Nikoleta, and as the bus passed Georgi, he went into the shop.

Suddenly Mallory's cellphone buzzed in her pocket. It sounded like an angry fly trapped behind glass, and both the noise and the sensation startled her. She wrestled the phone from her pocket and stared at it.

"What's going on?" Pete whispered.

"It's Bob," Mallory whispered. "But it's too risky to answer it." She held the phone on her lap for a while before she nudged Pete and gestured toward the back of the bus with a tilt of her head.

The bus picked up speed in a blast of exhaust as Mallory stumbled to her feet, and holding tight to the seat backs as she walked, she moved to the back of the bus. Pete followed her.

Mallory slid into the very last seat, Pete beside her. She still kept her voice low, though they were now many rows behind Nikoleta.

"I think we're safer back here," Mallory said. "Less of a chance of being discovered. Now that Nikoleta's brother is gone, she won't be so focused on him and might start looking around."

"So you think we can talk now?" Pete asked.

"Yes," Mallory said. "But we still need to keep an eye on Nikoleta. Maybe it's best if we keep our faces partly hidden."

"Should we hold something in front of them?" Pete asked.

"That would work," Mallory said. "But then we couldn't watch Nikoleta. Just so long as we don't keep facing forward, we should be O.K."

Mallory could see that Pete was looking pleased. "That was pretty amazing," he said.

"It sure was," Mallory said. "What a stroke of luck that they showed up outside our dorm and that you suggested we follow them."

"It's crazy what people will say when they don't think you're listening," Pete said. "I mean, all we had to do was sit there, and we've practically solved the case! Wait 'til Jupiter hears this!"

"I think he'll be pretty pleased," Mallory agreed.

"We learned how Dr. Stonebridge got set up, and who did it," Pete said, "and we learned that Mr. Dimitriou's estate manager is connected to the theft. What a way to repay Mr. Dimitriou for his kindness."

"And we also found out who's behind smuggling the tetradrachms into the country, and how they do it," Mallory said. "But we don't know who the two thieves were. And we don't know where the treasure is."

"That's true," Pete said.

As she talked to Pete, Mallory kept glancing out the window to see where the bus was going. She tried to remember the end of the route on the map she'd looked at earlier. They had left the crowded streets of Santa Barbara's commercial district behind and were now driving down a wide thoroughfare in what seemed to be a mostly residential neighborhood. In the distance, the sun glinted off the Pacific.

As if he could read her mind, Pete asked, "Do you know where we're going?"

"No," Mallory said, "but it looks like a pretty rich neighborhood."

The houses were set back further from the street, many of them hidden from view by landscaping. The bus stopped less frequently now, and no one was getting on. There were fewer and fewer people on the bus. Not only was Mallory feeling more conspicuous, but she was worried about what would happen when they got off.

"If we just start wandering around in a neighborhood like this," Mallory said, "we're going to stick out a lot."

"You can say that again," Pete said.

Then almost straight ahead, Mallory saw a tall circular white tower that looked suspiciously like –

"A lighthouse!" Pete said.

As they got a little closer, Mallory could see that they'd arrived, without knowing it, at Dimitri Dimitriou's oceanside estate. There was a two-paneled wrought-iron gate – not unlike the one at the entrance to the Salvage Yard – that stood open at the entrance. An asphalt drive wound down to the main cluster of buildings, all of which Mallory remembered from the photographs she and Jupiter had found in their library research.

It was unmistakable, a little Mykonos – the whitewashed guesthouse and main house, the small domed building, the stone walkways and gardens lush with bird-of-paradise and smoke trees, the separate island on which the lighthouse stood, the hundreds of feet of coastline. Tall palms rose into the blue sky, long, slightly bent trunks crowned with a host of feathery branches. But you wouldn't find those on Mykonos, Mallory knew.

It was even more beautiful and more imposing than in the photographs, Mallory thought. It really was as though they had turned a corner and found themselves in Greece.

Pete was staring, his eyes wide. "What a place!" he said. "It must belong to a movie star."

She turned to Pete, who hadn't seen the photographs. "Not exactly," she said. "This is Dimitri Dimitriou's estate."

"You're kidding me!" Pete said.

The bus came to a stop several hundred feet from the wrought-iron gates, and the few remaining people on board got to their feet. Including Nikoleta Kyriaku. This was clearly the end of the line.

"What should we do?" Pete asked. "Get off?"

"We could either do that, or we could tell the driver we made a mistake and we need to take the bus back into the city."

"What's the upside of that?" Pete asked.

"That's where Jupiter, Bob, and Rafael are," Mallory said.

"True enough," Pete said, "but wasn't Jupiter talking about coming out here to interview Stavros Economides?"

"No," Mallory said. "He was just going to call him and ask him to set up interviews with Achilles Kyriaku and that guy from ICE."

Mallory watched as Nikoleta walked up the aisle and carefully down the steps at the bus's front door. She didn't look back and clearly hadn't noticed them at all.

The bus driver turned around in his seat and shaded his eyes, looking back at them. They were the only ones left on the bus. "Are you kids getting off?" he asked.

"Well, what do you think?" Mallory asked Pete. "Head back to Santa Barbara or call Bob and Jupiter and then snoop around a bit while we wait for them?"

"Snoop around!" Pete said. "Let's go." He was on the aisle this time. He got to his feet and started toward the side doors. "We're getting off," he called to the bus driver. "Thanks!"

Mallory followed him. On the whole, she thought this was the right decision, but she hoped they weren't making a mistake.

12

Pete Has Suspicions

As Pete bounded down the steps, he took a deep breath of the air off the ocean – tangy, salt-laden, filled with ozone. His eyes took in the oceanside property, the winding drive and paths, the beautiful sun-drenched white buildings, and the vast glittering Pacific just beyond it with a sense of wonder. How great was this! he thought. Not to mention, surveillance at its best!

Having Stavros and Nikoleta walk by just after Pete and Mallory's call with Chris had ended had been a very lucky break. To have Chris tell them that ever since Nikoleta had been a young girl she'd been in love with a boy who'd been five or six years older than she was; to also have him tell them that when the man's wife had drowned in a sailing accident, Dimitri Dimitriou had brought him to California to manage his house and grounds; and to then see Nikoleta walking with Stavros Economides –

And not just walking with him, but floating around him in a haze of joy – well, it was a lesson in something or other, Pete thought. Chris saying Nikoleta had a 'crutch' on Stavros had reminded him of his own accidental conversation with Califia the day before, and now he was suddenly thinking of just how powerful that kind of feeling was.

Not love, exactly, but attraction.

And to have Nikoleta actually admit to her brother that she was a total pushover when it came to the men she loved – it had been interesting to hear that. From the other side, so to speak. Because, he, Pete, was also a bit of a pushover when it came to that sort of thing. And he was afraid that Dr. Stonebridge might be, too.

All afternoon he'd been feeling terrible about Dr. Stonebridge's situation and not knowing how to help. Now he knew that if worse came to worst, he and Mallory could testify as to what they had heard Nikoleta Kyriaku tell her younger brother. At least, he *hoped* they could, though he was afraid that what he and Mallory had heard might be called hearsay. And no matter what, Dr. Stonebridge was going to be pretty shaken up by what happened. He really thought Nikoleta had given him the bracelet because she liked him.

"Gee," Pete said to Mallory. "Do you

remember how many times Dr. Stonebridge said *no* when Jupiter asked him if he had a girlfriend or if there was anything between him and Nikoleta?"

"About six," said Mallory, "if I was counting right."

"So he'll be embarrassed that this is out in the open," Pete told her. "That he accepted the bracelet as a gift and invited her out for coffee the afternoon before the robbery. He clearly didn't want anyone to know that. And because what we heard was hearsay, he'll obviously have to tell the story himself − that she wanted to see the bracelet, that he took it off, and that she could easily have switched a new bracelet for the one he'd been wearing."

"Maybe not easily," Mallory said, "but that she could have managed it."

"Boy," said Pete, shaking his head. "Love can get really sticky."

Mallory smiled as if she understood what Pete was really thinking. "Sometimes" she said. "But sometimes it doesn't. And Califia really likes you, Pete. When she was telling me about the play she's in this summer − "

"A play about the Greek gods!" Pete exclaimed. He was afraid he might blush.

"− she said she remembered how nice

you were to her last summer after she found herself holding a real dagger in the tomb scene. She likes you, really."

This made Pete feel amazingly good but also embarrassed. As they walked along a hedgerow toward Dimitri Dimitriou's property, he tried to change the subject. "I wonder what this play 'The Gods' is all about," he said. "Califia said it was like a French farce. Do you know what that is?"

"A lot of people popping in and out of bedrooms. A lot of cases of mistaken identity," said Mallory. "And since the Greek gods are known, above all, for their *humanness*, I can see how they would work pretty nicely in that kind of play."

"The Greek gods are known for their *humanness?*" Pete asked, a bit incredulously.

"Oh, yes," said Mallory. "Zeus and Hera and Artemis and Apollo and Poseidon and Aphrodite and all the rest – they were always getting angry, and being jealous, and betraying people they shouldn't have betrayed. Not that you should betray anyone, really. But people do, all the time – so in Greece, the gods did, too.

"When Nikoleta – who Dr. Stonebridge liked and always treated well – got involved in this plan to make it look as though he'd been one of the robbers, she acted like a Greek god might have done in one of the myths," Mallory said. "The same goes for Stavros betraying the friendship and trust of Mr. Dimitriou, and Nikoleta and Georgi and the two other brothers back in Greece betraying their own brother Achilles."

"Yikes," Pete said. "That's a lot of betrayal. You'd think a bunch of gods would do better than that."

"Maybe," said Mallory. "But one thing I like about the gods of Olympus is the way that each one has a different kind of human personality. It made them easy to identify with, for the Greeks, I guess. The fact that their gods were flawed probably made them feel better about how flawed they were themselves. Of course, they were the ones who made up the stories to begin with. So they just copied their own behavior."

She stopped and pulled her cellphone out of her pocket.

"We'd better call Bob and Jupe to let them know where we are and what's going on," she said.

Pete watched as she dialed Bob's number and listened while it rang. Mallory's expression changed as soon as Bob picked up.

"Hey, Bob," she said. "It's Mallory." She paused. "Yes, I know you called. We were on a bus and I couldn't pick up." She listened for a minute and then asked Bob to hold. She turned to Pete. "They're back at the residence hall. Rafael had some stuff he needed to do back home, so he dropped Bob and Jupiter off and they were wondering what had happened to us."

"Tell them what we did!" Pete said. "Go on!"

"Bob?" Mallory said. "Could I talk to Jupiter, too?"

Both Bob and Mallory put their cellphones on speakerphone, and then Mallory filled Bob and Jupiter in, without going into every single detail. They'd seen Nikoleta Kyriaku walk by the dorm, followed her onto a bus, and overheard her talking to her brother Georgi, she said.

From that conversation, she and Pete had discovered that Nikoleta and Georgi were doing the coin smuggling, and that she and the estate manager, Stavros Economides, were behind the theft of the Minoan Treasure. They had also discovered that Nikoleta had helped to set up Dr. Stonebridge for the theft. Now they were outside Mr. Dimitriou's estate, Mallory explained.

"I think we should get over there and look around," she said. "We still don't know where the thieves stashed the treasure, and the sooner someone finds it, the better. Since we now know that Stavros Economides is in this up to his eyeballs − for all we know he master-minded the whole thing − with Mr. Dimitriou off in Greece, it makes sense that the thieves would have brought the treasure here. Since it's on the ocean it also makes sense that they're planning to put it on a boat before Mr. Dimit-riou gets back."

"If it's not gone already," Jupiter said tensely. "And if Nikoleta was headed out to Dimitriou's estate, why did she take the bus rather than come back with Stavros? After all, Dimitriou's estate is where he lives and works."

"I wondered about that, too," Mallory said. "The only thing that makes sense is that Stavros had something else to do first − some-thing important."

"O.K.," Jupiter said. "I'll buy that. But still, she could have just gone with him."

"Unless there was something else impor-tant that needed to be done out here, and that couldn't wait," Mallory said. "Anyway, this area has so many expensive houses that I'm worried someone will stop and ask us what we're doing here if we don't get out of sight."

"I wish I knew Dimitri Dimitriou's cell-phone number," Jupiter said. He sounded a bit annoyed. "I blame myself. I could have lifted it from Dr. Stonebridge's phone when we were in his study. If I had it, I could ask for his advice. After all, he knows all these people. But with him in Greece and Dr. Stonebridge in jail and the cops pretty much useless, I'm afraid it's up to us to decide what to do."

"What about calling the museum director?" Mallory asked. "Do you have his number? Was he helpful this afternoon?"

"Not particularly," Jupiter said. "He was cordial but not the sort of person I would turn to. Besides – " He paused and his voice got growly. "He's working with that agent from Immigration and Customs Enforcement – Hunter Baines – the one who Mr. Dimitriou mentioned. He seems to have a lot of faith in the man, but I wasn't impressed. In fact, there was something about Baines I distinctly didn't trust."

"O.K.," Pete said. "So now what?"

"Here's what we'll do," Jupiter said. "The bus you caught – Where did you get on?"

"On that road between the dorm and the ocean," Mallory said. "There's only one bus stop."

"So Bob and I will catch that bus and join you as soon as we can. In the meantime, you should go over to the estate and look around. Don't do anything sneaky. In fact, you should find Nikoleta Kyriaku. Remember that Mr. Dimitriou explicitly told us to contact his estate manager, so when you see her, that's all you need to say − that although we didn't exactly tell her the truth this morning, Mr. Dimitriou himself told us to ask Stavros Economides to set up interviews with Achilles Kyriaku and Hunter Baines."

"But that's a waste of time," Pete protested. "We already know Achilles isn't mixed up in this."

"Yes," Jupiter said. "And we also know that Hunter Baines would be no help at all. He wouldn't tell us anything. So it's just a cover story − so that you have a reason to be there in the first place."

"And for the two of you when you get here," Mallory said. "The advantage of the story is that it's absolutely true. We just leave out the part about not wanting to conduct the interviews any more."

"But how will we get out of here?" Pete asked, thinking ahead.

"When Bob and I board the bus," Jupiter said, "we'll call Rafael and tell him what the plan is. I'll arrange for him to come looking for us if he doesn't hear from us first." He paused and his voice changed. "Oh, and by the way, Pete, Bob and I just saw a statue of Aphrodite in the Museum of Classical Antiquities."

"Geez," Pete said. It wasn't like Jupiter to try to embarrass him.

"He's just kidding," said Bob. "We'll see you guys soon."

What was up with Jupe? Pete wondered as Mallory hung up.

"Let's get going!" he said. At least they had a plan.

"Just remember," Mallory said. "Don't act suspicious. We have a reason to be here — even if it's not exactly true any more."

Pete had felt quite tense while Jupiter was talking, but as he and Mallory walked through the gates at the property's entrance, he began to feel better. He glanced at his watch. It was 6:00 p.m. and the workday was over. The estate had been built into a hillside and the driveway fell away and turned to the left. The lighthouse cast a long dark shadow, growing longer as the sun moved toward the horizon.

Two gardeners were piling rakes and other tools into a wheelbarrow as Pete and Mallory approached. A van had pulled up next to them. In it were a young woman, who might have been a maid, and a teenage boy. Both of them and the gardeners looked Hispanic.

"Hola!" Pete said to one of them. "Me llamo Pete. Qué tal?"

The man, who looked to be in his thirties, wore a ball cap but he shaded his eyes anyway as he looked at Pete.

"Oye, chico," the man said. "Me alegro de que el trabajo haya terminado. Puedo ayudarte?"

"What did he say?" Mallory asked.

"He said he's glad that work's over," Pete told her. "And could he help us."

"Ask him where the estate manager lives," Mallory said.

Pete turned back to the man. "¿Me puede decir dónde vive el Sr. Economides?" he asked.

"Sí, sí," the man said. He pointed to a white building past the main house, near the end of the driveway. "Vive alli."

"Muchas gracias," Pete said.

"De nada," the man said before he

picked up the handles of the wheelbarrow and pushed it toward a gardening shed.

Pete and Mallory sauntered down the driveway, past the main house, the biggest building on the estate but still constructed in the style of the Greek islands. The door of the estate manager's house was open, as were all the windows, to catch the wind off the ocean. Pete peered in before he rang the doorbell.

In no time, Nikoleta Kyriaku stood in the doorway. She had changed out of her work clothes and now wore a lavender sun dress. She looked very pretty, Pete thought.

"Hello," Nikoleta said. "What are you doing here? Didn't I meet you just this morning at the Classics Department?"

"Yes," Mallory said. "You did." She paused. "Is Mr. Economides here?"

Pete knew Mallory was well aware of the fact that he wasn't; she must be stalling for time.

Nikoleta looked perturbed. "What do you want with Stavros?" she asked.

"Our friend Rafael Solares – he teaches Special Ed. Do you know him?" Nikoleta shook her head. "Anyway," Mallory went on, "he's a friend of Mr. Dimitriou, and Mr. Dimitriou suggested we ask Mr. Economides to set up interviews with Achilles Kyriaku and with the man that Immigrations and Customs Enforcement has assigned to the recent robbery."

Now Nikoleta looked alarmed. "Did he?" she asked. "This is the first I've heard of it. And why in the world would you want to interview Achilles?"

Pete couldn't think of a reason other than the one he knew was no longer true, so he just shrugged slightly and tried to look puzzled. So far, this wasn't going well.

"I really don't know," Mallory said. "Our friend Jupiter Jones is on his way, but he hasn't told us why he wants to talk to either man. Are you a friend of Mr. Economides?"

Nikoleta relaxed a bit. Pete could see that she was happy with her current situation and proud of what her hard work and single-mindedness had achieved.

"Yes," she said. "I am a friend, a childhood friend from Naxos, in Greece. Stavros isn't here right now and he won't be back for a while. He's taking care of some business in Santa Barbara. I'm sorry." She turned away as if to leave them standing there.

"That's O.K.," Pete said. "We'll wait."

"Maybe while we wait we'll just walk around this beautiful place," Mallory said.

"Mr. Dimitriou said we were welcome to take a look at anything we wanted to."

Pete gulped. Mr. Dimitriou had not said that, but he didn't think that Nikoleta was about to call him in Greece to double-check.

Nikoleta looked surprised, even annoyed, but then she gestured toward the outside.

"Sure," she said. "Look around all you want."

Great! Pete thought. He was ready to take her at her word. They walked back up the drive toward the main house looking for any-thing interesting. "Let's go down to the cove," he said, and Mallory agreed. They took their time, occasionally shading their eyes and look-ing back up toward the road for any sign of Ju-piter and Bob.

Pctc thought his first reaction had been right. What a place! Rocky outcrops marked either end of the property, and the shoreline swerved inland between them in a gentle curve marked by a white sand beach. The water near the shore was a light gray-blue but as it got deeper it turned a deep turquoise. To one side was a wooden dock on the end of a short pier that jutted out into the ocean. A single rowboat bobbed there, attached by a rope to the pier, but Pete could see moorings for bigger, ocean-going boats.

Further down the shore was a man-made island that you got to by crossing an arched stone bridge – an island just large enough to house the lighthouse that stood upon it. Mr. Dimitriou had clearly chosen the property for the unique aspects of the shoreline.

"Look at this sand!" Pete said. He was down on his knees, digging his hands into the beach. It was almost white, flecked with quartz, and very fine. He remembered what someone had said about smugglers being able to find the beach because it reflected the moonlight.

At the southern end of the cove, where the land rose again in a solid rock formation, Pete spied what seemed to be a dark mouth. A cave! he thought – and although he and caves had a checkered history, he thought it would be worth a look. He ran along the beach, gesturing to Mallory to follow.

The cave, as it turned out, was very shallow – only about ten feet deep – and its floor was sandy. It provided shelter from the sun, and clearly that was one of its attractions. A number of beach chairs stood folded against one of the walls, together with a small pile of towels. It was clear that even at high tide, this cave stayed dry.

Pete lost track of time as they explored, and when he paused to notice, he was surprised at how far toward the horizon the sun had fallen. Though he'd been having a great time exploring, he was disappointed that he and Mallory hadn't been able to discover anything that looked suspicious.

"Everything looks pretty normal," he said to her. "No special ops guys dropping from helicopters."

"It is a little odd," Mallory said. "I thought that Nikoleta must be coming back here to take care of something that needed to be done before her boyfriend got back."

"Yeah," Pete said. "That's right. I wonder what that was. She sure didn't look like she was in a hurry when she came to the door."

"Maybe she did whatever it was already," Mallory said. "Or maybe she hasn't done it yet."

They were near the arched bridge that led to the lighthouse and Mallory started across it. The bridge wasn't long – Pete saw it was mostly decorative – but it was still pretty nifty to look down into the Pacific Ocean from the bridge's high point.

Standing there, he heard the slap of waves against the hull of a boat, and he looked up to see a rather large yacht coming from the south and not that far offshore. When it passed the rocky outcropping, it veered landward, toward Mr. Dimitriou's property. It was hard to see, because Pete kept getting blinded by the setting sun, but he shaded his eyes and watched as the motor cut off and the boat, on its own momentum, coasted up to the dock.

Just as the boat was being tied up, Pete turned to see Nikoleta Kyriaku burst out of the back door of the caretaker's house. She looked wild in her hurry, her long dark hair streaming behind her in the offshore wind, and she seemed a little panicked. She ran right up onto the pier and down it to the dock. Something was finally happening, Pete thought, and it looked suspicious!

"Ignore her," Mallory counseled. "Pretend you didn't even see her. We better make it look like we're not interested in her at all."

"What do you think's really going on?" Pete asked.

They watched as Nikoleta stood on the dock, her arms gesturing dramatically, and then stepped aboard the yacht and disappeared into the wheelhouse. From what Pete could see, there were two men aboard.

"Come on," Mallory said. "Let's go into the lighthouse and stay there until Nikoleta leaves the boat."

The exterior door to the lighthouse stood open. Pete and Mallory walked inside to find themselves in a large room. It was a good deal more dim inside than out, even though there were two windows – one looking seaward and one landward. Both had heavy tight-fitting wooden shutters that could close them, when needed, from the outside. Mallory pointed them out and mentioned that they would have to be closed by hand when a big storm blew through; at least that was the way it was done throughout the Mediterranean, she said.

The room was round, of course. To one side stood a thick wooden door that fit snugly into its doorjamb. It had hardware for a padlock, though it wasn't locked. Pete saw the padlock, nearby, hanging on a hook. He opened the door, which led to the wooden stairs to the light.

Pete craned his neck, staring up, but he could see nothing but the under-treads of stairs. As the building rose, it became distinctly more narrow until the entire interior space was nothing but a winding wooden spiral staircase that ascended around a thick solid wooden column.

The lighthouse's walls were lined with vertical boards, painted white. In fact, as far as Pete could see, the entire lighthouse was a miracle of woodworking.

"Spiral staircases everywhere," Mallory said. Pete knew she was referring to the stairs that had descended into the treasure room at Castello Serreno – their last case.

"Yeah," Pete said, "but whoever built the lighthouse had no choice but to do it this way."

The bottom section, where they stood, had room for a couple of folding chairs and two big wooden storage boxes locked with padlocks. On the wall, two pairs of binoculars hung from hooks.

"Let's go up," Pete said. He and Mallory grabbed the binoculars and started to climb the stairs. Around and around they went. It was a strange experience and a bit dizzying, one step after the next. Halfway up, there was a window on the ocean side. From that height, and with the binoculars, they could see far out, and though the surface of the ocean had seemed untroubled from the ground, they could now see a number of boats speeding here and there, leaving white trails in their wake. Off in the distance, Pete spied what looked like a Coast Guard vessel.

When they got as high as they could get, Pete could see they still weren't quite all the way to the top. Above them was the beacon itself, surrounded by Fresnel lenses. Pete remembered the other lighthouse in these parts, built on a protruding headland north of Santa Barbara sacred to the Chumash. Rafael had taken them all out on his boat to see it, but they'd had to turn back because the ocean was too rough.

"Remember what Rafael said about that other lighthouse we never got to see?" he asked.

"You mean the one on Point Conception?" Mallory asked. "It wasn't really about the lighthouse, though. It was about the point of land."

"That's right," Pete said. The headlands had been known to the Chumash as the Western Gate, the place where the souls of the dead leapt off the earth and entered heaven.

"I just hope we won't be encountering any dead souls around here," he said.

"I see no reason why we should," Mallory said. "Unless we're very unlucky."

Pete peered down at the dock far below, then raised the binoculars to his eyes. Nikoleta Kyriaku was still on board the yacht, he thought, unless she'd managed to get ashore

when they were climbing the stairs. He focused
on the prow of the boat. There, in painted letters, was the name LUCKY LADY. He lowered
the binoculars.

He wondered when Jupiter and Pete
would arrive. Granted, it was a long bus ride,
but shouldn't they have gotten here by now?
And when would Stavros Economides get
back?

Pete stared out to sea, thinking about
Stavros's story. "I wonder if Mr. Economides's
wife really died in a boating accident," he said.
"Maybe it wasn't an accident."

"Don't let your imagination run away
with you," Mallory advised.

"I won't," Pete said. "But we really don't
know. He's shaping up to be a pretty bad guy.
Who knows what else he might have done?
And where *are* Bob and Jupiter, anyway? Do
you think they're going to be O.K.?"

13

A Very Unfortunate Car Ride

At about the moment Pete wondered this, Bob was wondering the same thing – and a little more intensely. After he'd put his phone on speaker as he and Jupiter sat on the couch in their suite in the Senior Residence Hall, he'd listened carefully to the conversation between Mallory and Jupiter, and now his head was spinning with what Pete and Mallory had found out. He was astounded.

"How can we find the bus schedule?" Jupiter asked him. "We have to get out to Mr. Dimitriou's as soon as we can."

"I'm sure it's online somewhere," Bob said, "along with a map of the routes. Do you want me to look it up?"

"Yes," Jupiter said.

Bob grabbed his laptop from the table where he'd dropped it, and once he'd booted it up, he soon found the map. There were a lot of buses and a lot of bus routes, but it was easy to find the one that started near the Henley Gate on the Santa Barbara campus. It wound through the city proper and ended in a residential district on the coast. Bob pointed to the terminus.

"That must be where Pete and Mallory are," he said.

It looked like quite a distance.

"What about a timetable?" Jupiter asked.

Bob noted the number of the bus route and then matched that with the bus's running times.

"It runs every half hour," Bob said. He glanced at his watch. "It looks like we just missed one. The next one's in about twenty-five minutes."

Jupiter looked annoyed. Bob knew well that when Jupiter took the bit between his teeth he wanted to move forward quickly, and this latest news would frustrate him.

"I know how we can use the time," Bob said. "It's not as though Nikoleta Kyriaku or anyone else is going to feed us once we're out at Mr. Dimitriou's. Why don't we pick up some sandwiches to take with us?"

"But we're on campus," Jupiter said.

"Let's go to the dining commons where we had breakfast. It's very close – just over by the lagoon."

On the way to the commons, Bob

thought about what they'd seen at the museum. Jupiter had been struck by the statue of Aphrodite, but as they'd headed to the director's office, he himself had been impressed by a statue of a noble woman who he'd read was Clio, one of the nine Greek muses. She was holding a set of tablets and a scroll, and, as the Muse of History, she seemed to be staring into either the past or the future. It had made Bob think how interested he was becoming in the study of history. Maybe Clio would turn out to be his muse.

Bob was happy to see that he had been right about the dining commons. They stuffed a paper bag with a wide variety of ready-made sandwiches and added some apples and bananas for good measure. As they headed toward the bus stop, Bob felt oddly hungry, but he agreed with Jupiter that they should wait until all four of them were together. He turned his mind away from the sandwiches and toward what Mallory and Pete had discovered.

"It's hard to believe that Mr. Dimitriou's estate manager is behind the theft," he said.

"Hard to approve of," Jupiter said, "but not hard to believe. It makes sense that it would be an inside job, so to speak."

"What do you mean?" Bob asked.

"It's disappointing but true that most crimes are committed by people close to the center of a case," Jupiter said.

"And in this case, it's good news for Dr. Stonebridge," said Bob.

"Yes and no," said Jupiter. "Unless we can find the actual treasure and restore it to him and Mr. Dimitriou, the victory will be decidedly muted."

Yes, Bob thought. Dr. Stonebridge would be relieved to be released from jail, but it was he who had helped discover the treasure, he who had literally dug the treasure from the ground, and he who had helped persuade the Greek government to loan it to the museum. Even if his reputation was cleared and he didn't wind up being blamed for the theft, unless the treasure was returned, its disappearance would haunt him for the rest of his life. And he would also have to face the fact that he'd been betrayed by a woman he'd allowed himself to have feelings for – but who he'd been a fool to trust.

"So," Jupiter said. "Pete and Mallory were quite right to want to start looking around Mr. Dimitriou's estate. It's logical that that's where the thieves have stored the treasure. We need to find it. After all, Dr. Stonebridge is our client in this case, and what matters to him must matter to us. Though he's not in a position to communicate with us right now, I am sure his foremost concern – even more than his own release – would be the recovery of the treasure."

By this time, Bob and Jupiter had reached the bus stop and had seated themselves on a bench in the shade of the metal overhang. Bob glanced at his watch. The bus wouldn't be there for another ten minutes.

Just then a shiny black blunt-nosed SUV pulled into the parking lot next to the bus stop. Bob was startled to see the Immigration and Customs Enforcement logo on the side of the car – a circle with the American eagle in the center clutching arrows in its talons, the words in gold arrayed around it.

Hunter Baines got out. His brow furrowed and he put his hands on his hips, pushing his sports coat back and revealing his ICE badge.

"What are you two doing here?" he asked. He was clearly surprised and his voice was threaded with suspicion.

"We're waiting for the bus," Jupiter said pleasantly. "We're staying in that residence hall over there." He pointed across the road.

Baines didn't turn to look. Both Bob and Jupiter got to their feet and came out from under the bus shelter. The sun was quite hot.

Bob had known that Baines was tall when they'd met him earlier. But now that he was standing, he could see how tall he really was − over six feet, and thin. Bob was struck by how people with Baines's body type all looked a bit alike. It occurred to him that if he'd seen him from the back, Bob might have mistaken him for Bob's father. Or Dr. Stonebridge.

"This is a bit peculiar," Baines said, "running into the two of you twice in a single day. Who are you, anyway? What's your interest in this theft? Why not leave it to the professionals? These are probably dangerous men we're dealing with. If you're not careful, you could get hurt."

Bob looked at Jupiter; it seemed that, at the same time, they had both concluded that honesty was the best policy when it came to dealing with people who worked for the government.

"We were introduced to you earlier," Jupiter said, "so I won't repeat our names. We're two members of a professional detective firm called The Three Investigators and we're on an assignment. Dr. Godwin Stonebridge and Mr. Dimitri Dimitriou have asked us to investigate the theft of the Minoan Treasure and to help out in whatever way we can. When we met you earlier, we were in the museum to view the CCTV tapes of the robbery, after Mr. Dimitriou called Dr. Dare to arrange that."

Baines's eyes narrowed. "What help could *you* possibly be?" he asked.

Bob could see that the information had put Baines off-balance and that Jupiter was pressing his advantage. "Actually," Jupiter said. "Mr. Dimitriou gave us permission to go talk to his estate manager, Mr. Economides – to ask him to arrange interviews with Mr. Achilles Kyriaku. And with you, Mr. Baines."

"With me?" Baines said. His voice communicated both astonishment and outrage. "Whatever do you think I could tell you?"

The sun was in Baines's eyes, and he reached up to the crown of his head where he'd placed his dark aviator sunglasses – the type Bob supposed were issued to every enforcement agent along with their name tag. As he did, his wrist shot out of his jacket's sleeve. The glimpse of his wrist stunned Bob. It looked a lot like the wrist wearing the silver bracelet in the CCTV tapes he and Jupiter had seen earlier. The wristbone was prominent and, if he was seeing right, there was a triangle made of three large freckles.

Of course, he was probably seeing things, but the very idea that he might not be made him feel instantly self-conscious and awkward. Unlike Jupiter and Mallory, who managed to maintain their cool in tense circumstances and who were both able to pretend to be people they weren't when the occasion called for it, Bob was a terrible liar and an even worse actor – as he had reflected just the other morning. The harder he tried to hide something, the more likely he was to give it away – and the minute he imagined that it was this guy, Hunter Baines, who had been wearing the bracelet in the tapes, he felt his words stick in his throat. The smile he had plastered on his face *felt* like plaster – forced and artificial and a dead giveaway.

Baines seemed to notice the change in Bob immediately. "What were you staring at?" he asked Bob.

"Who, me?" Bob said. "Nothing. Nothing. Nothing."

Jupiter looked at him in consternation.

"You were looking at my wrist, weren't you?" Baines asked, his voice with an edge that could cut.

"I – uh – ," Bob stuttered. "I was just noticing that you weren't wearing a watch. Usually guys like you wear watches, don't they? I mean, you need to know if it's more than a freckle past a hair, don't you? Pacific elbow time."

It was a terrible joke, as old as the hills. Bob had heard it first in third grade when he'd thought it was clever. That time was long gone. Nobody laughed, and Baines actually looked offended.

Jupiter decided to step in. "What my friend means – " he said.

"Why this bus stop?" Baines asked. "Where are you going?"

"Actually," Jupiter said, his voice calm and even. Bob could see he was trying to deflect Baines's attention from whether Bob had been staring at his wrist. "Our research indicates that this bus will take us close to Mr. Dimitriou's estate. As I said, we were hoping to speak to Mr. Economides."

Baines's eyebrows twitched. He'd put his sunglasses on, so his face was a mask, but his body, which had tensed, relaxed. But his voice still had an edge to it when he said, "If that's where you're headed, then you're in luck. I'm about to head out to the Dimitriou estate myself. In fact, I'm expecting the estate manager you mentioned, Stavros Economides, to swing by and pick me up any minute. There should be room in the car for the two of you."

Jupiter looked surprised at the news. "Thank you very much," Jupiter said. "How long have you known Mr. Economides?"

Baines tensed again. "What do you mean?" he said. "I just met him."

"Why is he picking you up, then?" Jupiter asked.

"Listen, kid," Baines growled. "Do you want the ride or don't you?"

It would be convenient, Bob thought, but he wasn't at all sure that it would be safe. Clearly Baines was offering them a ride in order to keep an eye on them. Bob's tongue-tied and stricken demeanor had made him suspicious. But it was more and more clear to Bob − and maybe to Baines himself − that Baines's reaction had given him away. Almost certainly Baines was one of the two thieves he and Jupiter had seen on the CCTV tapes.

As Bob was thinking this, another SUV − this one a bright shiny blue − came speeding down the road, braked, pulled up next to Baines's, and parked. The man who got out looked very Greek to Bob. He was medium height with broad shoulders and a straight narrow nose, his skin olive, his hair dark and curly.

He could have been an athlete when he was younger, Bob thought. He could still be. He looked quite fit. He was pretty good-looking but the scowl on his face masked that. He had a brushy mustache. When he took off his sunglasses, Bob saw that his eyes looked a little shifty, and there was a smudge or shadow under his right eye. Bob edged a little closer. Just under Economides's right eye Bob could see a little scar – just like the scar under the eye of the second man in the CCTV tapes!

His pulse racing, Bob realized he was looking at the two men who had stolen the Minoan Treasure. He felt like someone had grabbed him by the throat and wouldn't let go.

Of course, he'd already known, from what Pete and Mallory had said, that Stavros was behind the theft and had used Nikoleta Kyriaku to set up Dr. Stonebridge. But he hadn't known that the man had actually been one of the thieves, and it was very different to suddenly see the evidence for himself and to realize simultaneously how badly equipped he was to hide what he now knew.

It was almost too much to process –

Economides had once worked for the Greek Ministry of Culture, and Baines now worked for the U.S. government to recover and return smuggled antiquities to their countries of origin. But rather than protect the things they'd been hired to protect, these guys were the two thieves who had betrayed and abused their positions and were responsible for the theft of priceless and irreplaceable ancient objects. Maybe that's why Stan the IT guy had been so cynical about government employees, Bob thought − because his life experience had taught him there was every reason to be!

"Mr. Economides," Baines said − a fake and formal address Bob saw was an attempt to disguise the fact that these two were as thick as − well − thieves − "I offered these two boys a ride out to Mr. Dimitriou's estate with us. Mr. Dimitriou suggested they talk to me, and that you could arrange an interview for them with Achilles Kyriaku."

There was no way that this could be code, Bob knew, but somehow something else was being communicated between the two men. The smile on Economides's face seemed sinister as did his false heartiness when he said, "But of course! Why should they wait on a bus when we are going there directly?"

He turned to Bob and Jupiter, looking very much to Bob like the wolf in Red Riding Hood's grandmother's clothing. "Hop in!"

He gestured to the car he had just arrived in with an expansive sweep of his arm.

Bob attempted to get Jupiter's attention so he could shake his head no, but Jupiter was already getting in the back seat. Baines stood, his arms folded on his chest, until Bob climbed in next to Jupiter, and then he got into the passenger seat next to Economides. The key turned, the engine roared, and Bob heard the solid *thunk* as the automatic door locks engaged. He swallowed hard.

As the car got underway, Bob decided to keep his mouth shut. There was nothing he could do but make the situation worse, so he sat as Jupiter tried to make halting conversation with the two men who, it quickly became clear, preferred to ride in stony silence.

Bob looked around the interior of the SUV, which was surprisingly clean, as though it had been recently wiped down and vacuumed. He glanced over his shoulder into the luggage compartment behind him. His breath caught in his throat. There were two duffel bags back there. Bob closed his eyes and sank down in the seat. They looked just like the duffel bags on the CCTV tapes. Well, if The Three Investigators' task had been to find the stolen treasure, it looked as though the case was over.

Only it was far from over, Bob knew. He and Jupiter were now, essentially, captives.

The ride took far longer than Bob had expected, and he found it hard to concentrate on whatever was flashing by outside his window. Economides had the air conditioning on HIGH, and Bob shivered, unsure whether as a result of the temperature or his own anxiety.

The cellphone in his pocket called out to him, but it was far too dangerous to pull it out and try to use it. He and Jupe had planned to call Rafael when they first got on the bus, but it was too late now. He couldn't even call Pete and Mallory to warn them. He thought it was best if he just let it be. He'd need the cellphone later, and if he didn't call attention to it, he could hope that Baines and Economides wouldn't think of it and wouldn't taken it away when they got to the estate.

All of a sudden a different cellphone rang in the front seat. Economides took it out of his pocket and glanced at it before gesturing to Baines.

"I'd better take this," he said. Baines nodded and Economides held the phone to his ear.

"Nikoleta," he said. "Hold on, glykiá mou." He said a few more things but it was all Greek to Bob. As he talked, he braked smoothly and pulled over to the side of the road before getting out and walking away from the car to talk privately.

While he was gone, Baines turned around, his eyes hidden behind his black glasses. "How is everything back there?" he asked – a question that might have been friendly if it hadn't sounded so threatening.

What were Stavros and Nikoleta talking about? Bob wondered. Bob knew it was important, whatever it was. Soon enough Stavros returned to the car and slid behind the wheel. Economides turned to Bob and Jupiter. "It seems your friends have gotten there before you." His tone was as neutral as he could make it, but it still seemed very threatening.

"Yes," Jupiter said. "Mr. Dimitriou said it would be all right if they went out."

"Of course it's all right," Economides said. "We would wish you to be no other place. You will be our guests." He smiled at Baines.

Uh oh, Bob thought. He didn't like the sound of that. He nudged Jupiter who bristled. He flashed a fixed smile at Bob and warned him to stay quiet with a quick brisk shake of his head.

"Everything under control?" Baines asked Economides.

"Perfect," Economides purred before the engine roared to life.

It seemed that, after the call, it took almost no time for them to get to the Dimitriou estate, but Bob was so pumped with adrenaline he didn't really know. As they drove through a set of wrought-iron gates weirdly reminiscent of the gates at the Salvage Yard, Bob was taken aback by the sheer beauty of the place. The Pacific glittered with gold scales as far as the eye could see and the cluster of white buildings they approached was washed with gold light. Bob wished he could have seen it under happier circumstances. At the moment its otherworldly beauty carried a touch of menace.

Economides drove slowly down the winding drive, past lush landscaping and rough stone walls, past what Bob presumed must be Mr. Dimitriou's house, before parking before a smaller dwelling near the bottom of the drive. He and Baines got out, as did Jupiter. Bob touched his cellphone in his pants pocket for good luck, then climbed out too, taking the bag with all the sandwiches and fruit. He had lost his appetite, but he didn't want to leave the bag in the car.

In the distance, now that he was at sea level, he could see how close the sun was to the western horizon. Economides stood close to Baines and said something Bob couldn't hear. Then he turned to Bob and Jupiter.

"My girlfriend told me that your two friends are at the top of the lighthouse watching the sunset. Perhaps you would like to join them?"

"That sounds like a good idea," Jupiter said.

"Then, afterwards," Economides went on, "when it is getting darker, you can all come up to the estate house. Will you be hungry?"

"No," Bob said, clearing his throat. He raised the paper bag he was holding. "We brought dinner."

"You young people think of everything," Economides marveled. "Anyway, when you come, you can talk to Mr. Baines, ask him anything you want. Yes?" he said, turning to Baines.

Baines gestured as if he had no choice in the matter.

"And I will set up an interview for the four of you for tomorrow with Mr. Achilles Ky-

riaku. Good?" He smiled, flashing a set of very
white teeth.

"Thank you," Jupiter said,

Baines went back to the car and grabbed
a small bag from the front seat. He nodded to
Economides, who then auto-locked the doors,
leaving the two duffel bags in the back.

"Come, then," Economides said.
"Follow me." He led the way down a grassy
slope to an arched stone bridge that led to the
small island that held the lighthouse. Bob noticed that Baines stayed back, to bring up the
rear, with Jupiter and him between the two
men. Bob was feeling more and more uneasy,
but there didn't seem to be anything he could
do about what was going on.

They crossed the bridge in single file and
went around to the ocean side of the lighthouse. Way up, almost at the top, Bob could
see two small figures on a circular lookout surrounded by a chain link cage. He knew the
metal mesh must have been installed for safety,
but under the circumstances it made the lighthouse look like a watchtower in a high-security
prison.

As he watched, he could see one of the
figures start waving. "Bob! Jupiter!" Pete's
faraway voice called. "I was wondering when

you were going to get here. Who's that with you?"

"I am Stavros Economides, Mr. Dimitriou's manager," the man called up. "Why don't the two of you come down so that I can introduce myself properly?"

"O.K.," Pete called. He and Mallory disappeared inside the tower.

Bob, Jupiter, and the two men had barely managed to get inside when, amid a huge amount of banging and stamping, Pete and Mallory came down the stairs and burst into the room.

"What a view from up there!" Pete said enthusiastically. "You guys have to see it!"

"Just a minute, young man," Stavros Economides said. "You must slow down and be more careful. The stairs are narrow and go around and around. There is nothing to stop you if you start falling."

In Bob's state, this piece of good advice sounded suspiciously like a threat.

"I'm sorry," Pete said, nodding. "I'm Pete Crenshaw and this is Mallory MacLeod."

Mallory looked less enthusiastic than Pete; in fact, she looked rather cautious as she also nodded at the men.

"We are very pleased to make your acquaintance," Economides said. "I wish we had time to know you better, but we must be going."

As Bob watched, Economides casually lifted a padlock off a hook it hung from and swung it on his finger before turning and locking the door leading up to the lookout. The padlock's click was loud and final.

"I thought you said we could all go look at the sunset," Bob said.

"I did," Economides said mournfully, "but I forgot that tonight is the night each week when the lighthouse lights up. No one is allowed into the top when the light is about to come on. It is far too hot and bright to be around it. Too dangerous. You will have to come back some other time to watch the sunset."

"The sun sets every night," Baines said. He had his back to the exterior door. "So you can come back any time."

"We live pretty far away," Pete said.

"That is too bad," Economides said as he inched his way around the room.

All of a sudden Baines stepped backwards through the door and Economides followed him. Before Bob or any of the others could react, they had slammed the wooden exterior door shut, and in the shocked silence that followed, Bob could hear a deadbolt slide into place.

"Wait!" Pete yelled. "What's going on?"

He rushed to the window that faced the sea just in time to see a maliciously grinning Hunter Baines close and bolt the exterior wooden shutters. Bob whirled to the landward window to see that Stavros Economides was closing and bolting that one too.

In a frenzy, Pete rushed the door and threw himself against it. It didn't budge.

"Oww!" he said as he bounced off and started rubbing his shoulder. "Bad decision."

Though the room had been dim before, with the windows shuttered and bolted, now it was downright gloomy. Bob saw that what little light remained came from the ocean side — where the sun was about to slip beneath the edge of the world. Then the four of them would find themselves in total darkness in a small room at the bottom of a lighthouse on a tiny artificial island.

They were trapped!

14

Stolen Treasure, Headed West

Jupiter was startled by the speed with which everything happened at the end, but if truth be told, he wasn't really surprised. The thieves hadn't had much choice if they wanted to get away with the loot, and by the time Stavros Economides got the telephone call from Nikoleta Kyriaku, Jupiter had known that he and Baines understood The Three Investigators were on to them.

As he stood in place, waiting for his eyes to become accustomed to the dimness, he was aware that his friends were all talking at once. Pete ran to first one window and then the other to see if he could rattle the shutters loose, while Mallory and Pete both reached in their pockets for their cellphones.

He had thought of that, and he'd been intrigued by the fact that neither Economides nor Baines had searched them or tried to take their phones away. Of course if they had, it might have been more difficult to trap the four of them in the lighthouse – after all, there were only two bad guys. But they clearly hadn't been worried that Jupiter, Pete, Bob, or Mallory would be able to call someone.

"You call 911," Bob said to Mallory. "I'll call Rafael. Is that what we should do, Jupe?"

"That would make sense under normal circumstances," Jupiter said. "But I'm pretty sure you won't be able to get through."

"Why?" Pete asked. "Isn't the signal strong enough here?"

First Mallory and then Bob took the phones away from their ears. Bob stared at the little lighted screen. "It says 'Out of Service,'" he said. "What does that mean? We know Rafael's number isn't out of service."

"That's what I get too," Mallory said. "911 is out of service? I don't think so." She turned to Jupiter. "How did you know?" she asked.

"I had a suspicion that Baines would be using a cellphone jammer," Jupiter said.

"But they're illegal!" Mallory said.

"So is stealing priceless antiquities," Pete said, "and that didn't stop them."

"I don't know how I knew that," Jupiter said. "I picked it up somewhere."

"Yeah," Pete said, "along with everything else in the Encyclopedia Britannica."

Jupiter smiled. "Anyway," he said.

"Here's a conundrum. It's illegal to manufacture cellphone jammers in this country, and it's also illegal to operate them. But it's not illegal to own one."

"What good does it do to own something you can't use?" Bob asked.

"I don't know," Jupiter said. "But I seem to remember reading that federal officials are allowed to use them when they're working on a case. Hunter Baines is obviously a criminal, but he's also a federal employee working for ICE, so I'm sure he had access to one."

"So he's jammed Bob's and Mallory's phones!" Pete exclaimed.

"I also seem to remember that small cellphone jammers can fit in a pocket and are good for a distance of seventy feet or so," Jupiter said. "Do you remember when Baines went back to the car, Bob?"

"You think he was getting a jammer?" Bob asked.

Jupiter nodded. "If he turned one on and set it outside that door, it would jam Bob's and Mallory's phones for as long as the battery lasts. Quite a long time, I'm afraid."

"Jeez," Pete said. "How are we going to get out of here? And it's getting so dark I can't see my hand in front of my face!"

What Pete said was true. The faint light that filtered through the shutters was growing fainter. Jupiter could see his own body, but Mallory, Pete, and Bob were slowly fading into the darkness. They had to decide what to do.

"We'll get out eventually, of course," Jupiter said. "Economides and Baines clearly don't want to risk actually hurting us, or holding us hostage, so someone will find us fairly soon. By tomorrow Rafael will come looking, or someone who works on the estate will walk by." Jupiter realized with a sinking feeling that Rafael didn't exactly know where they were. The phone call they had planned to make to him had been eclipsed by the appearance of Baines and Economides.

"But tomorrow will be too late, I'm afraid," he went on. "By then the Minoan Treasure will be gone. Right now − if my eyes don't deceive me − it's sitting in two duffel bags in the back of Economides's car."

"It was right there in the car with you?" Pete yelped.

"Pete and I think they're planning to take it away from here in a boat called the *Lucky Lady*," Mallory said.

"Just before we went up in the lighthouse, a big yacht tied up at Mr. Dimitriou's dock, and we saw Nikoleta Kyriaku come running out of the manager's house," Pete said.

"Nikoleta ran right down the pier and onto the dock to greet the men on board," Mallory said. "She was clearly waiting for them."

"And they'll escape with the treasure," Jupiter said. "Baines, Economides, and Kyriaku, all three of them. It would hardly be wise for them to stick around in California after what they've done."

"And after they know we know they've done it," Bob said.

"So we better get to work," Jupiter said. "At least they didn't tie us up. That was lucky. But luckiest of all is that I've got my Swiss Army knife with me."

"You always have it with you," Pete said. "But how is a Swiss Army knife going to get us out of here?"

"You remember the day I made you practice using the tiny tension wrench I retrofitted the knife with?" Jupiter asked.

"Sure, Jupe," Pete said, "You made us practice for so long, I bet I could pick a lock in the dark."

"Exactly," Jupiter said.

"You taught us a tension wrench isn't

enough," Bob said. "We also need a pick."

"Unfortunately, you're right," Jupiter said. "Fortunately, when you and I were in the museum, I nervously picked up a paperclip. It's still in my pocket, I believe." He thrust his hand into his pants pocket, suddenly worried. "Yes," he said, relieved. "It's still there."

"But the door has a deadbolt," Bob said. "I heard it click shut."

"I wasn't thinking of picking that lock," Jupiter said. "There's no way we can get out of the outside door." In the darkness Jupiter pinched his bottom lip. "But if we pick the padlock at the bottom of the stairs, we should be able to get out onto the lookout where Pete and Mallory were earlier. Am I right?"

"Yes," Mallory said. "But it's a long way down. What were you planning on doing?"

"Yelling would do no good," Jupiter said. "The staff is gone for the day, which means that the only people left on the estate are the crooks. They're hardly going to help us."

He pinched his lip harder. "Let me think," he said.

"Is there some way we could use the beacon?" Bob asked.

"I'd almost forgotten," Jupiter said. "Tonight's the night it goes on – and

Economides said it's dangerous." Suddenly his plan was beginning to fall apart.

"Well, surely we can turn it off," Bob said. "All we need to do is find the electrical box."

"Or maybe we can turn the light off and on," Mallory suggested, "to send a signal. When Pete and I were up in the lookout, we saw a Coast Guard ship patrolling. If we could signal to them, that might work."

"I've got an idea," Pete said excitedly. "Maybe we can use the light to send an SOS! Just the other day I was talking to my father about Morse code, and I remembered how Bob and I used our walkie-talkies. But all we really knew was SOS. You know the whole code, don't you, Jupe? Or you did!"

"Yes," Jupiter said. "I memorized it years ago, and unfortunately I rarely forget anything."

"Fortunately, you mean!" Pete said.

"But I don't see offhand how we can convert a beacon that huge, and that's set to its own pattern, to send Morse code," Jupiter said.

"Its own pattern?" Pete asked.

"Each lighthouse has its own code – its identification signal," Jupiter explained, "so that boats at sea will know which lighthouse they're seeing. Besides," he added, "since the beacon is undoubtedly run by a computer these days, it's even more of a problem. We don't have the knowledge, skill, or tools to reset it. And even if we could shut it down, how would we start it up again to use it as a signal?"

"From the electric box?" Bob asked.

"I'm afraid that would be too cumbersome," Jupiter said. "I don't think we could send any sort of signal that way."

"I hate to say this," Pete said, "but does anyone have a candy bar or anything? I'm starving."

"I'm glad you brought that up," Jupiter said. "I'm quite hungry myself, and I'm happy to report that Records and Research thought ahead and got everyone dinner."

This was followed by a lot of whooping, most of which came from Pete. "Way to go, Bob!" Mallory said.

They sat together on the floor in a small circle. Jupiter could barely make out his friends as Bob opened the bag he'd brought and handed out sandwiches and fruit. Then there was quiet, except for the sound of everyone chewing, and carefully sharing the water in the two water bottles.

Jupiter had known he was hungry, but

he'd had no idea he was *that* hungry. He found himself with an egg salad sandwich, not his favorite, but it was gone before he knew it, together with a banana. After the refuse, banana peels, and apple cores were all carefully collected and put back into the paper bag, Jupiter felt a rush of energy. He'd surveyed the room carefully when they'd first entered it, and now with his brain back in gear, it suddenly occurred to him that there might be something useful in those padlocked wooden boxes he'd seen along the wall.

"Time to get to work on these locks," he said.

"Locks?" Mallory asked.

"I thought I ought to check out these storage chests," Jupiter said.

He got out his Swiss Army knife and levered open the tension wrench. Then, carefully, he felt around for and retrieved the paperclip from his pocket and unbent it so that it would serve as a pick.

"Can we help, Jupe?" Bob asked.

"Thanks," Jupiter said. "But as you'll remember, this is a one-man job."

"We'll just stand here and give you moral support," Pete said.

"Great," Jupiter said. "But don't stand

too close."

It was so dark now that he was doing everything by feel. He found the key slot on the bottom of the padlock and inserted the tension wrench, putting the slightest pressure on it in the direction the key would turn. Then he inserted the paperclip above it and began carefully to rake the pins inside. One by one, he felt the pins click into place. The last one took some doing, but he was patient and kept at it until the final pin set, and the weight of the padlock itself made it drop off the bail.

"Got it," Jupiter said.

"Good going, Jupe!" Pete said.

With that success under his belt, Jupiter made quick work of the padlock on the second chest. Meanwhile Pete and Bob were rummaging in the first one.

"I found a saw," Pete said. "Ouch! It's sharp!"

"Maybe we can saw our way out," Mallory said.

"And a hammer," Bob said. "What are these?" He pulled out two long black cylinders. "Flashlights?"

"Bingo!" Pete said. "And there are two more – smaller. One for each of us.

"Here," Jupiter said. "Give me one of

the big ones."

Bob handed it to him and Jupiter fumbled in the dark, sliding his hand up the shaft until he found the switch. He pushed with his thumb and the room was flooded with blinding light. "Wow!" Pete said. "That's bright!"

"It's a halogen bulb," Jupiter said. "Whatever you do, don't shine it in anyone's eyes. Unless one of the bad guys shows up. Bob, does that one work?"

Bob switched it on. They had two very bright, very powerful flashlights.

Then Jupiter found the button on the flashlight's side. "Wait!" he said. "What's this?" He pressed it and the light flashed on. When he released it, the light turned off. He tapped it and let go immediately. On-off. It was fast. "There's your Morse code," he said. "And these are bright enough to carry a good distance. We're in business."

"Now all you need to do is pick the last lock," Pete said.

"Would you like to do the honors, Pete?" Jupiter asked.

"No, thanks," Pete said. "You're a genuine certified lockpicker!"

Bob turned his flashlight on but kept it focused well away from where Jupiter worked on the last lock. In the light, it was easier. As soon as the padlock released, he told Bob to turn off the light.

"Let's go!" Pete said.

"Wait," Jupiter said. "We won't go up until it's totally totally dark – "

"It is!" Pete said.

" – and until we have reason to think the yacht with the Minoan Treasure on board is about to leave the dock. We don't want to tip our hand. The first thing we ought to do is see if we can cut off electricity to the beacon."

In the light from the flashlight they found the electric box. It had been painted white and almost disappeared into the white wall on which it had been fastened. Jupiter studied it until he found the lever than connected several circuits and pulled it down. That would take care of the beacon.

While he was doing that, Bob tried his cellphone again. "It's still jammed," he said.

Then, "Listen!"

Everyone froze. In the distance, Jupiter heard the sound of voices. They were too far away to be able to make out what they were saying, but there were several of them, a jumble of male voices and a single female voice. There seemed suddenly to be a good deal of activity down at the dock. Feet pounded on the pier. One of the men shouted. Then Jupiter heard an outboard motor burst into life and shut off. There was more talking, people calling to one another, and then the engine came to life once more.

"Here we go," Jupiter said tensely. The motor made a distinctive sound in reverse as the yacht backed away from its mooring, a low rumbling that changed pitch when the turn had been completed and the bow was pointed toward the open ocean. The noise now was higher, throatier, and louder.

"They're off," Jupiter said. He had come up with a plan while picking the final lock and shutting off the lighthouse's beacon. "Here's what we'll do. All four of us will climb up to the lookout, and then we'll take up our positions at the four corners of the compass. That way we'll be just below the beacon, which is where anyone looking at the lighthouse would expect to see the light. Two of the flashlights aren't as bright, but they'll have to do. That way we can cover the entire field of view. Whether a person's on a boat or on land, we'll have a good chance of catching their attention."

"That is, if they know Morse code," Bob said.

"Don't be so gloomy!" Mallory said. "Everyone knows SOS, and surely someone will think it's pretty strange that it's being broadcast in four directions simultaneously."

"I'll go first," Jupiter said. "Bob, would you turn one of the smaller flashlights on so that we can see where we're going?" Bob gave the other bright flashlight to Pete and he and Mallory took the smaller ones. When he'd turned it on, Jupiter was gratified to see that it was quite bright – if not with the blinding intensity of the halogen bulb. It bounced off the walls of the spiral staircase, illuminating the treads.

Jupiter started up – slowly at first. The stairs were tightly wound and after the first ten or fifteen, all he could see below him were stairs – no longer could he catch a glimpse of the room where they'd been. It felt a little claustrophobic, actually. The breath caught in his throat and he felt a little dizzy. But he didn't say anything and kept climbing and soon he had gotten into the rhythm. Below him he could hear the sounds of his friends' feet climbing.

At last he reached the top and walked out onto a round metal balcony surrounded by a mesh cage. Though he appreciated the safety the cage gave, at that point he wouldn't have minded at all to be face to face with the darkness of the night. Mallory, Pete, and Bob clustered next to him. Out to sea, he could see a boat heading west, its signal lights small against the vastness of the ocean, the Minoan Treasure on board. Down to his left, the lights of the compound cast a dim glow. And off behind him, the sky was lit by the lights of Santa Barbara.

"Ready?" Jupiter shouted. "Let's start with S – O – S. That's three quick dots – *dit-dit-dit* – followed by three longer dashes – *dah-dah-dah* – and then another *dit-dit-dit*. The *dahs* are supposed to be three times as long as the *dits*."

"You keep talking like that," Pete said, "and I'm going to start laughing."

"No laughing," Jupiter said. "Just ditting and dahing. On my signal. Ready. Set. Go."

Jupiter had picked the spot on the circle that looked directly seaward. Pete was to his left, pointed south down the coast, Bob was to his right, and Mallory was directly opposite him, pointed landward.

Jupiter pressed the button on the flashlight's shaft, three times, quickly, then held the button down three slightly longer times, then three more quick presses. Dit-dit-dit, dah-dah-dah, dit-dit-dit.

He repeated it. Again. And again.

He squinted out across the water, trying hard to see if there was any motion, anyone at sea who seemed to have noticed. There was nothing. The boat with the Minoan Treasure continued westward. No one had turned toward land.

Maybe an SOS wasn't sufficient, Jupiter thought. Maybe a more specific message was necessary. "O.K.," he yelled. "Let's try something different. How about STOLEN TREASURE HEADED WEST? Followed by SOS."

"Great," Bob yelled. "But you have to give us the commands."

Jupiter started yelling out *dits* and *dahs* even as he started sending out the signal himself. It was quite difficult, really, remembering what letter came next and yelling out instructions on the code for that letter, and pressing the button on his flashlight. After he'd done it a half a dozen times, he felt exhausted.

But he kept at it, and his comrades did too, all of them standing tall, backs straight, with military precision sending out a signal into the darkness of the night. STOLEN TREASURE HEADED WEST.

When Jupiter took a break, everyone came rushing to him to see if he was all right. "I'm fine," Jupiter said, stretching his neck. "I just need a minute or two."

"Boy, you can say that again," Pete said. "This is hard."

"We have to keep at it," Jupiter said. "It's our only hope. Or not exactly our *only* hope, but our only hope that the treasure will be rescued and the crooks caught."

He was secretly worried that the flash-lights' batteries would give out. He didn't know if he was imagining it, but it seemed to him as though the beam his flashlight threw was a little less stark, a little less bright than it had originally been. And of course, he had no way of knowing how much charge the batteries had had to begin with.

He looked out to sea. The stars were beginning to brighten, and the signal lights on the yacht bearing the treasure away had disappeared. Then the moon rose behind them, throwing its own silvery light across the waves.

"We can't give up," Jupiter said. "Take your positions." He began calling out instructions again. And again.

"My flashlight just died," Bob said. "It's as bright as a firefly."

"Mine too," Mallory said, The two of them had joined Jupiter, both of them disappointed and upset.

"Pete," Jupiter called. "Come stand right next to me." Pete had the other bright flashlight and Jupiter hoped that, if they doubled the strength of the signal they were sending, that someone at sea would notice and respond.

"Let's get into a rhythm and see if we can synchronize our signal," Jupiter said. "Two flashlights are better than one. O.K. Begin! Dit-dit-dit dah dah-dah-dah."

He started spelling STOLEN. Then TREASURE HEADED WEST SOS.

"What a team!" Mallory said. "You're doing great. I bet they can see that in Hawaii."

Bob started laughing. "Or wherever," he said.

Jupiter's head was pounding, and the finger he was using to press the button was beginning to cramp. He realized he didn't have very much left in him.

"Wait!" Pete cried suddenly. "What's that?"

Jupiter looked closely and saw the signal lights of a good-sized boat. As he watched, the lights seemed to get brighter.

"Someone's coming," Bob said. "Look!

They're headed right for us."

Jupiter redoubled his efforts. He'd gotten a whole new burst of energy, especially when he saw, as it came closer, that it was a Coast Guard patrol boat. It was compact and looked like it was very capable of a high-speed chase. The American flag flew from its mast.

The boat slowed as it approached land and maneuvered easily to dock at the end of the cove where the yacht had been before. Jupiter let his arms fall to his sides. He wondered if they'd ever been so tired. Pete and Mallory and Bob were cheering, jumping up and down, pumping their fists. He watched as a man in a white uniform ran down the pier, across to where the stone bridge began, and over it to the lighthouse's island.

He looked up, bent backwards at the waist, cupped his hands around his mouth and yelled. "Are you all right up there?"

"Don't worry about us," Jupiter called down. "Did you get the message?"

"STOLEN TREASURE HEADED WEST," the man called.

"That's right," Jupiter said. "The Minoan Treasure. Priceless. Stolen from the Santa Barbara Museum a couple of nights ago. It's on a yacht. It left from here maybe an hour ago. You've got to intercept it."

"It's called the LUCKY LADY," Pete yelled down. "If that helps."

"That helps a lot, young man. Thanks," the man said. "We're on it."

He started toward the bridge.

"Before you go," Jupiter said, "could you pick up the cellphone jammer that one of the thieves left? It should be right outside the door." He shone the beam of his flashlight down toward where he thought the jammer probably was.

The Coast Guardsman kicked at the dirt and then hunkered down. He picked up something and waved it at Jupiter. "Got it!" he said. "I'll keep it as evidence."

"Thanks," Jupiter said. "Now get going!"

"Yes, sir," the Guardsman said, saluting. "With your permission, sir, I'll notify the police so they can come and get you out of there."

Jupiter laughed and saluted back. "Permission granted. Thank you, sir."

The man turned sharply and broke into a run. Jupiter watched him as he dashed over the bridge, across the shoreline, down the pier and back onto his patrol boat. In no time at all, the engine was engaged, the boat had backed up, and was storming over the ocean in pursuit of the thieves.

"Boy!" Pete said. He looked at Jupiter slyly. "That boat is fast! And we got them, sir!"

Jupiter smiled and slapped him five.

15

A Hellenistic Hoard

Three days later, Pete and Rafael were sitting together in Rafael's backyard, talking intently, while Bob, Jupiter, and Mallory were a little distance away, with Elena. In a little while, the six of them would be heading for Little Mykonos where Pete and his friends would meet Dimitri Dimitriou for the first time, and afterwards Rafael would be driving them back to Rocky Beach. He'd picked them up there this morning. For now, Pete was absorbed in their conversation.

"What do you mean by a red telephone?" Pete was asking.

Rafael laughed. "That's right," he said. "You're probably too young to know that during the Cold War, the President of the United States and the Premier of the Soviet Union had a kind of hotline to send secure communications to one another via transatlantic cable.

"There was never an *actual* red telephone," he went on, "but when the movies got their hands on the idea, they turned it into a special red telephone on the desks of the

President and the Premier. When I was a little kid, and my mother took me to Mass, I used to wonder why God didn't have a red telephone on his desk so that we could talk to him anytime we wanted to.

"In those days the only phones were landlines," he added, "so I imagined picking up a bright red, heavy handset with a cord every time I went into the confessional at my church. I don't think I could ever have imagined a conversation with God on a cellphone. On a cellphone, you could talk to God *anywhere* – even in the bathroom! – and that would clearly have been very disrespectful."

"I'll say!" said Pete. "I felt funny even talking to Califia just sitting on the steps of the office at the Salvage Yard, and she's just a god in a *play*. There's something about talking on a cellphone that I can't warm up to. In fact, if I had *my* way, they'd all be jammed, forever!"

Rafael smiled at Pete's fervor. "So you like this girl a lot, then?"

"I *think* I do," said Pete. "But I don't know how you can know a thing like that, really, before you – well, you know – "

"Yes," said Rafael, quite soberly. "And the problem is that, even then, things don't always work out the way you want. My wife and

I were married for seven years, and had a son together, before we decided we weren't really compatible. She was much more ambitious than I was. Elena and I are better suited to one another."

"Elena was great about Dr. Stonebridge," Pete said. "I can't believe she got the police to make a formal apology for arresting him. And she did it so quickly! Usually that sort of thing takes forever — if it ever happens at all."

"It almost never does," said Rafael. "But you four are the ones he should really be thanking. And *me*, maybe, for having asked you to investigate what was going on with him to begin with," he joked.

"We had a lot of luck," Pete said. "And it might have been easier if he'd told us the truth about his feelings for Nikoleta Kyriaku."

"Sometimes people just can't do that," Rafael said, smiling. "Besides, I'm sure Godwin was simply embarrassed at the difference in their backgrounds and ages. But with you and Califia, there should be no problem."

Pete was really grateful to Rafael for sticking with the topic. It felt easier to discuss it with him than with his friends.

"But I get the sense she's pretty ambitious, too," he said. "Like your ex-wife, maybe. She was great in *Romeo and Juliet* last summer and this summer she's playing Aphrodite. I didn't even know who Aphrodite *was* until Mallory told me. She also told me the Greek gods were all pretty human. That they were always getting angry, and being jealous, and betraying people. She said that she liked the way each one has a different kind of human personality. You remember when you looked at the reproduction Alexander coins and decided there should be one for each of the four of us?"

"Of course," said Rafael. "Mallory was Alexander the Skeptical, Jupiter was Alexander the Brilliant, Bob was Alexander the Careful, and you were Alexander the Courageous."

Pete felt embarrassed being reminded of that – especially because he really hadn't done anything all that courageous on this particular case.

"Well," he went on, "maybe the Greek gods were sort of like that. Each one representing a different aspect of normal people. They were almost a horde, really."

Rafael laughed. "That's an odd word to use about gods," he said.

Normally Pete would have blushed, but right now, talking with Rafael seemed so natural that he didn't.

"Well, the thing is," he said, "I've been thinking. Bob's been using the alphabet to organize our cases. He's gotten to H, and since the Greeks had a lot of gods, and Dr. Stonebridge told us that Greek culture after Alexander is called "Hellenistic," I was thinking that maybe this case could be called *The Mystery of the Hellenistic Horde.*"

Rafael looked at Pete curiously.

"That's an interesting idea," he said. "Though I'm not sure the Greek gods deserve to be called a *horde*. The Greeks were very precise in the way they divided up reality. They knew the difference between one thing and another better than almost anyone else – the difference between men and women, and love and hate, and reason and feeling. Aphrodite was the goddess of beauty, love, desire, and pleasure, while Zeus was the god of the sky, weather, law and order, and justice. The precision with which they thought led to a lot of great things – like the lighthouse you and the others signaled to the Coast Guard from!"

Pete remembered that Rafael had mentioned earth, air, fire, and water the day they'd met on the road in Rocky Beach, and how much Rafael had liked the idea that all things were made of just those four classical elements.

"Our friend Chris Markos told us that everyone in Greece loves lighthouses," Pete said. "He said that the ancient Greeks believed that the four elements of the world came together in a lighthouse."

"That's nice," said Rafael. "I didn't know that. But I can see it. A lighthouse is built on earth, right next to water, reaches high into the air, and burns fire. Or did in the old days, when they had to carry wood to the top!"

Just then, Elena got up and came over to where Pete and Rafael were sitting.

"I think we'd better get going," she said. "We don't want to be late to Mr. Dimitriou's lunch."

"No, we don't," said Rafael, climbing to his feet. "And we can arrive in style today because we're going in Elena's van."

As the six of them headed for the van and climbed in, Pete thought about the fact that Mr. Dimitriou had returned from Athens less then twenty-four hours after the thieves had been caught by the Coast Guard – the Minoan Treasure intact in the wheelhouse of the *Lucky Lady* – and in the two days that had passed since then, he'd accomplished an amazing amount – including organizing this thank-you lunch.

The museum director and Stan Bloomberg – the IT guy who had shown the CCTV tapes to Jupiter and Bob – were both going to be there, and so were Dr. Stonebridge and Achilles Kyriaku – Nikoleta's brother and the manager of Mr. Dimitriou's business.

Pete assumed that Mr. Dimitriou would tell all of them the latest news about the Minoan Treasure and the villains who'd tried to steal it.

Once they arrived at his estate and parked, Pete watched as the man himself walked out the door of his home and descended the steps to greet them. He was tall and tan and handsome, with bright dark eyes, and thick curly black hair. He looked confident and relaxed – wearing a dark sports jacket over a white shirt open at the neck – and seemed very friendly.

In fact, he opened his arms as if he wished to embrace them all.

"Welcome!" he said. "We meet at last." He shook everyone's hand with both of his, his grip firm and decisive.

"Thanks so much for inviting us!" Pete said.

"Invite you?" Mr. Dimitriou said. "There

would be no celebration if it weren't for you! My friend Godwin might still be in jail and the great treasure he found gone forever. I am not sure which part of the story I found most remarkable, but perhaps it is that the Coast Guard told me that when you first started signaling from the lighthouse, they were inclined to ignore you. A prank, they thought, from private land, over which they have no jurisdiction, and which isn't their business. But when you sent the actual message – STOLEN TREASURE HEADED WEST – it became their business. How is it that you knew Morse code?"

"Jupiter knows almost everything," Pete said.

Jupiter cleared his throat. "I studied it some years ago," he said, "and I never forgot it. But it was really Pete's idea."

"Well, young man," Mr. Dimitriou said, turning to Pete. "You saved the day, not to mention some priceless artifacts."

Pete turned crimson in an instant. That was nice of Jupe and Mr. Dimitriou, he thought, but he really hated to be praised in public. And it had just been an idea. "Thank you," he said. "I mean – "

"So," Mr. Dimitriou said, "a happy happy day, with a few dark clouds." An expression of regret and sadness crossed his face, and Pete thought he knew why.

"I'm sorry about your friend," he said. "We heard the story about how you tried to help him, and others from Naxos."

"It can't be easy when someone you trust betrays you," Jupiter said.

"No," Mr. Dimitriou said. "It is a shame but not a total surprise. Even when we were boys on Naxos, Stavros had sticky fingers. I thought he had reformed. I am afraid he used Ms. Kyriaku's infatuation with him to drag her into the business."

"What's going to happen to her?" Mallory asked.

"Between her brother Achilles and me," Mr. Dimitriou said, "we managed to convince the police not to press charges. Her only crime, after all, was switching one cheap bracelet for another, and I asked the sergeant to find that law in the books and show it to me."

"But what about the smuggling?" Bob asked.

"That actually never came up," Mr. Dimitriou said. "The police were so focused on the robbery that the tetradrachms eluded them. The Kyriakus' scheme, of course, is now ancient history, and the coins they didn't manage

to sell will be returned to the Greek government.

"Achilles and I agreed that handing his brother and sister over to the American police was not a good idea. Of course they are both being deported, and it is likely that all the Kyriakus will face charges back in Greece. But if so, I will do my best to convince the Greek *asty-nomía* that Nikoleta was an unwitting tool of her brothers."

"I'm glad to hear that," Mallory said. "Because I think she really was. What about Economides and Baines?"

"They've been charged with grand larceny and smuggling, as well as impersonating police officers and unlawful confinement of the four of you and the museum guards," said Mr. Dimitriou. "And that's not all. Because Baines was an ICE agent, he's also being charged with misusing his position, blocking your cellphones, and forging papers to make the treasure salable."

"What kind of papers?" Pete asked curiously.

"The papers stated that the various items, all described and accounted for on the manifest, had been legitimately sold to Stavros Economides," Mr. Dimitriou said. "The yacht

312

they were on was supposed to rendezvous with another boat in northern California, and that boat was to take Economides, the papers, and the treasure back to Greece.

"Baines was planning to quit his job and join his partner," Mr. Dimitriou continued. "They were going to sell the treasure to a very wealthy Greek businessman and collector — a man as wealthy as I am, but totally lacking any sense of honor. But of course The Three Investigators scrambled their plans quite dramatically.

"Their original plan was to leave Nikoleta behind and pin the whole thing on her, which was why it was easy to convince the police simply to deport her — they could see how she had obviously been set up to take the fall. But at the last minute, with you four locked in the lighthouse, they took her with them. They were afraid she might let you out, or give them away," Mr. Dimitriou concluded.

By now, his other guests had arrived and were walking toward where Mr. Dimitriou had been standing talking with The Three Investigators and Rafael and Elena.

Mr. Dimitriou waved in the direction of the new arrivals.

"But that is all over now," he said, "and

we must look to the future. First, the luncheon. And tomorrow the exhibit will reopen at the museum, with tighter security. In a strange way, since this has ended happily, it has been the most astonishing publicity. I can hardly imagine the crowds that will come to see the treasure that was stolen and then returned."

Soon, the six of them were saying hello to Dr. Stonebridge, Pete and Mallory were being introduced to Stan Bloomberg and the director of the museum, and all of them were meeting Achilles Kyriaku. Pete could see right away that he was a quiet and methodical man – the sort who would make a good manager, and not at all dramatic or mercurial like his younger siblings.

He was also so clearly embarrassed at the shame they had brought on the Kyriaku name he hardly knew what to say. He could not apologize enough about the smuggling or the robbery. And he blamed himself – he should never have suggested hiring Georgi, and somehow the entire episode with the tetradrachms had escaped his attention. He spoke to Mr. Dimitriou in the most abject tones.

"Enough, Achilles," Mr. Dimitriou said. "You are certainly not responsible for your brother or sister, and if you judged their characters incorrectly, then what am I to say about me and Stavros, who was the worst of them all? Of course it is very sad for you that Nikoleta and Georgi let you down so badly, but you have done nothing wrong. You have always been a model of honor, and I owe you my life. Come, let's go eat."

Soon after that, they were sitting at a table set in the shade on a stone patio which looked out on the Pacific, glittering in the sun.

As Pete tucked into the delicious first course, he reflected that what could have been a big disaster, and an international incident, really *had* had a very happy ending. All of a sudden, Mr. Dimitriou turned to where The Three Investigators were sitting. Pete had imagined that he had already said everything he had to say to them, but he had been wrong.

"What you did, you four, is bigger than you think," Mr. Dimitriou said. "You have rescued an innocent man and have returned to humankind a treasure from over thirty-five hundred years ago. This deserves not only recognition but a reward. I was wondering – "

A reward! Pete thought.

Jupiter interrupted. "We're grateful for your kind words, Mr. Dimitriou," he said, "but there's no need for any reward. We love to solve mysteries, and we were more than happy to help. Besides, Dr. Stonebridge was really our client."

Bob and Mallory joined Jupiter in thanking Mr. Dimitriou but refusing his offer – but Pete had a thought he liked at once.

"Mr. Dimitriou," he said. "You've been very generous to the people of Naxos, and we know someone there who could use some help. His name is Christos Markos and we met him a couple of years ago when he helped us with a case here in the United States. But he was also a great help on this case. He was our eyes and ears on the ground in Naxos.

"He gave us information about the Kyriaku family we couldn't have gotten anywhere else – and also about your ex-friend Mr. Economides," Pete added. "He and his father are trying to run a diving shop in Naxos Town, right on the harbor. But sometimes business isn't good and Chris's father has trouble paying rent on his shop. Instead of giving us anything, maybe you could help them pay for the rent or something."

"What a generous idea, Pete," Mr. Dimitriou said. "Everyone should have friends like you. If you give me the Markos's address, I'll be delighted to help them."

Mr. Dimitriou paused. Then he smiled. "But I still think that the four of you deserve a proper reward," he said, "and if you won't accept it from me, I hope you'll accept it from the Greek government. The Ministerial Council wants to award you a formal certificate of appreciation, as well as an honorarium in recognition of your having saved the Minoan Treasure from the thieves."

"Wow!" said Pete. "A formal certificate from the Greek government!" And an honorarium, too! he thought. "We'd love that, wouldn't we, guys!"

Lunch went on, and after dessert came coffee. At that point, the adults got deep into a conversation about local Santa Barbara politics, and at some point, after noticing that The Three Investigators had all fallen silent, Mr. Dimitriou suggested they might like to take a walk down to the ocean – or see the lighthouse again – and they all got to their feet and headed for the cove.

It was a beautiful summer day, mostly cloudless, with a cool breeze off the ocean. Passing boats left spreading Vs of foam in their wake. Far out, Pete saw a sailboat catch the wind. The door to the lighthouse was open, and with one accord, the four of them walked into it and looked around. The shutters were open, and so was the door to the spiral stairs, but instead of instantly ascending to the top, they all seemed to want to talk. They settled down on the floor, with their backs against the wall.

"I'm really glad you told Mr. Dimitriou about the Markos's dive shop," Bob said.

"Me, too," Pete said. "Although Chris isn't that much older than we are, he's already been working hard all his life. So have we, I guess, but not like *that*."

"I wish you hadn't said I know almost everything," Jupiter said. "This case has really brought home to me just how little I actually do know – about the Greeks, among a lot of other things. It's really astounding how many areas of our daily life the Greeks influenced – science and art, philosophy and politics, even sports – and how many things they invented."

"I *know*," said Pete. "Rafael told me that the Greeks invented libraries and theaters, and Dr. Stonebridge told us that they invented arched stone bridges, the catapult, the water-wheel, plumbing, and central heating – not to mention democracy!"

"And also the spiral staircase and the lighthouse," said Mallory. "I wish I'd had a chance to see one of the old ones, that burned wood."

"Rafael just mentioned that, too," Pete said. "Can you imagine how much trouble that was? Carrying wood all the way up? Did they keep it burning all the time, or just light it at night?"

"All the time, I think," Mallory said. "During the day all you could see was the smoke, but at night, when it was dark, you could see the fire. I really like what Chris told us about the ancient Greeks thinking a lighthouse was a perfect representation of the four classical elements. And you know what, guys? This morning I figured out that so are *we!*"

"What do you mean by that?" asked Jupiter.

"Well," said Mallory, "I was thinking of how we'll all be turning fifteen in a few months, and how our birthdays are all lined up in a row. August, September, October, November. Then it occurred to me that we each had different astrological signs."

"That's right," Pete said. "Jupiter's a Leo, Bob's a Virgo, I'm a Libra, you're a Scorpio."

"Yes," Mallory said. "But we never realized before how different signs are connected to the four elements. Leo is fire, Virgo is earth, Libra is air, and Scorpio is water!”

It took a minute for that to sink in. “Wow!” Pete said. “How cool is that?”

“Very cool,” Mallory said. “But what I want to know is what this case is going to be called!”

Bob smiled. “I was thinking ‘Hellenistic Hoard,’” he said.

“That’s just what I told Rafael!” Pete said. ‘A horde of Greek gods!”

“No,” Bob said, smiling. “The other kind of hoard. The one that refers to a collection or supply of stuff that's carefully guarded,” Bob said.

“Like the Minoan Treasure?” Pete asked.

“Kind of,” said Bob.

“But if I’m remembering right,” Jupiter said, “the Minoan period was considerably *before* the time of Alexander the Great's death – after which Dr. Stonebridge told us came the Hellenistic period.”

“That’s right,” Bob said. “But I was thinking more metaphorically. The Hellenistic hoard could be the inventions and ideas that Alexander spread across the world. I mean, if a hoard is a treasure trove, what's more of a treasure trove than a set of world-changing inventions and ideas?"

"Great thinking," Jupiter agreed.

Damn! thought Pete. That was sure better than his horde.

"But all your titles have a literal meaning as well," Mallory said. "Which is what makes them work."

Bob nodded. "I was thinking it could also stand for the tetradrachm Mallory found in the barrel at Aegean Treasures – and all the others that are still buried in Greece."

That about wraps it up, Pete thought.

"But what about a memento?" he asked. "We still need a memento."

"I offered the real Alexander silver tetradrachm to Dr. Stonebridge," Mallory said. "But he said we should keep it. And we still have the four reproductions. Along with the real one, they would be a great memento."

"Yes!" Pete said. "That's perfect! The four of us can be both the four Alexanders and the four elements! And I have another great idea. Let's go up to the viewing platform before the sun gets much lower."

He was genuinely happy with the way the case had come out, but on the way up the spiral stairs, Pete couldn't help but give one last thought to the conversation he'd had with Rafael before they'd left his house for Little Mykonos.

Granted, his idea – that since ancient Greece had a lot of gods, you could almost call them a *horde* – hadn't been the greatest he'd ever had, but all of a sudden he was having one he liked a lot. The fact that Greek inventions and ideas had been spreading from country to country as history had gone on seemed to suggest – at least to Pete! – that ideas were as much like a conquering army as they were like a treasure trove.

What he meant by that, he thought as he reached the lighthouse's deck, was that (for example) the ancient Greeks' idea that each individual mattered and should have a voice in the way their government was run could be seen as a sort of battalion trying to defeat the idea that they didn't, and shouldn't.

It was great to be in the open air again, looking toward the sea, glittering in the sun, and as he and the others stood in silence on the platform, shoulder to shoulder, Pete followed his thought to its end – that while you could certainly say that the ideas of the ancient Greeks had been treasured by lots of people who'd lived since the time of Alexander, you could also say that those ideas had taken the world by storm – the way an army could overwhelm an opponent. After all the years that had passed since the Greeks had shaped the world, that was pretty amazing.

Of course, a lot of things about life were amazing, Pete reflected. Like the fact that he and Bob and Jupiter and Mallory were standing here in silence, shoulder to shoulder, on the platform of an Aegean lighthouse – the Three Plus One Investigators – and the fact that, according to Mallory, Califia García-Williams might actually be interested in getting to know Pete better.

At the least, she had sounded impressed when he'd told her about getting trapped with Bob and Chris Markos in an underwater cavern when they were down in Florida that time. She'd even said she wanted to hear the whole story about Skeleton Island someday.

Maybe later that summer he'd find a way for the two of them to hang out together, and he'd tell it to her then. If only he had a red telephone he could use to call God up and ask him what the odds were.

No, that was stupid, Pete thought. God didn't know the future any more than Pete did. He'd just have to wait and see what happened

– though at least he could be ready if something did. Although he still didn't feel he really deserved to be compared to the coin Bob had ended up calling Alexander the Courageous, he *did* think he might deserve to be compared to a coin called Alexander the Ready-for-Anything!

ABOUT THE AUTHORS

Elizabeth Arthur

Elizabeth was born on November 15, 1953 in New York City. She is the daughter of Robert Arthur, the creator of The Three Investigators series. She was educated at Concord Academy in Concord, Massachusetts, the University of Michigan in Ann Arbor, Michigan, Notre Dame University of Nelson, British Columbia, and the University of Victoria in Victoria, British Columbia.

Before she started working on the New Three Investigators series in December of 2018, Elizabeth spent most of her life writing for adults. *Island Sojourn* – a memoir about building a house on a wilderness island in northern Canada – was published in 1980 by Harper and Row. A second memoir, *Looking For The Klondike Stone*, was published by Knopf in 1992. She is also the author of the novels *Beyond the Mountain, Bad Guys, Binding Spell, Antarctic Navigation,* and *Bring Deeps*.

Elizabeth's writing has received fellowships, grants, and awards from the Bread Loaf Writer's Conference, the Ossabaw Island Project, the Vermont Council on the Arts, and the

Indiana Arts Commission. She twice received fellowships from the National Endowment for the Arts and was the first novelist ever given an Antarctic Artists and Writers Operational Support Grant from the National Science Foundation.

Her novel *Antarctic Navigation* was chosen by the New York *Times* as a Notable Book, received a Critics' Choice Award from the San Francisco *Review of Books*, and was chosen as a Best Book of 1995 by *A Common Reader*. In 1996 the novel received the Ohioana Book Award for Fiction from the Ohioana Library Association.

Elizabeth has also taught creative writing at Miami University in Oxford, Ohio; the University of Cincinnati; and Indiana University/Purdue University of Indianapolis, where she directed the creative writing program. She and Steven Bauer met in 1980 at the Bread Loaf Writer's Conference and have been married since June of 1982.

Steven Bauer

Steven was born on September 10, 1948 in Newark, New Jersey. He was educated at Hanover Park High School in East Hanover, New Jersey, Trinity College in Hartford, Connecticut, and the University of Massachusetts in Amherst, Massachusetts. In 1970 he received a B.A. with Honors in English from Trinity, and in 1975 he received an M.F.A. in English from the University of Massachusetts.

Steven is the author of three books for young people – *Satyrday*, 1980; *The Strange and Wonderful Tale of Robert McDoodle*, 1999; and *A Cat of a Different Color*, 2000. His book of poems *Daylight Savings* was published by Gibbs Smith in 1989 and won the Peregrine Smith Poetry Prize.

Steven's work has received fellowships from the Bread Loaf Writer's Conference and the Fine Arts Work Center in Provincetown, Massachusetts. In addition, he has been given grants and awards from the American Library Association, the Parents' Choice Foundation, the Ossabaw Island Project, the Massachusetts Arts Council, and the Indiana Arts Commission.

From 1979 to 1982, Steven taught literature and creative writing at Colby College in Waterville, Maine. From 1982 to 2009 he taught at Miami University in Oxford, Ohio where he directed the graduate and under-graduate creative writing programs. In 2010 he established Hollow Tree Literary Services, an independent editing business.